My Heart's In The Highlands

100 Poems Dedicated to the Poetic Plateau Called Qinghai

诗的高原

歌咏青海的最美现代诗（汉英对照）

宋江涛　主　编

马　非　副主编

黄少政　译

马克·特雷迪尼克　廖美珍　审　校

青海人民出版社

图书在版编目（CIP）数据

诗的高原：歌咏青海的最美现代诗：汉英对照 /
宋江涛主编；马非副主编；黄少政译 .-- 西宁 : 青海
人民出版社 , 2022.6
ISBN 978-7-225-06361-4

Ⅰ.①诗… Ⅱ.①宋… ②马… ③黄… Ⅲ.①诗集—
中国 —当代 —汉、英 Ⅳ.① I227

中国版本图书馆 CIP 数据核字（2022）第 094338 号

责任编辑　崔　茜
责任校对　田梅秀
责任印制　刘　倩　卡杰当周
装帧设计　杨敬华　闫冬雨

诗的高原（汉英对照）

——歌咏青海的最美现代诗

宋江涛　主编

马　非　副主编

黄少政　译

出 版 人　樊原成

出版发行　青海人民出版社有限责任公司

西宁市五四西路 71 号　邮政编码：810023　电话：（0971）6143426（总编室）

发行热线　（0971）6143516 / 6137730

网　　址　http://www.qhrmcbs.com

印　　刷　陕西龙山海天艺术印务有限公司

经　　销　新华书店

开　　本　787mm×1092 mm　1/16

印　　张　19.5

字　　数　300 千

版　　次　2022 年 7 月第 1 版　2022 年 7 月第 1 次印刷

书　　号　ISBN 978-7-225-06361-4

定　　价　198.00 元

序言

吉狄马加

我曾经在祁连山下，看见过一群羊羔，它们的双腿全部下跪着，在吮吸妈妈的乳房。它们的行为让我感动。于是我将这种感动写成了诗。在青海高原的岁月里，令我感动的岂止是一个场景！置身于青海高原，大到浩瀚江河湖泊、圣殿般的雪山、穿越云霄的雄鹰，小至一顶草原中的帐房、一株岩石上生长的雪莲、一个老阿妈瘦弱的身影，都是诗的表达。所以我曾说，青海就是一座诗的高原。这也是我创办青海湖国际诗歌节的缘由。

生活在高原的先民，当然是最早歌咏这片土地的人。民间传承的古歌、山歌、谣曲，以及英雄史诗等，都为高原的身躯和灵魂注入了浓厚的诗意。而作为文人

PREFACE

Jidi Majia

Once we were driving on a road at the foot of the Qilian Mountain and a few lambs came in sight, all crawling, sucking at their mother's breasts, a behavior all too natural for mammals, but somehow I felt there was a sermon or lesson to be derived from within it. So I composed a poem in my head. It turned out that in my eight-year stint on the Qinghai Plateau, scenes of such reverential deference and gratitude for nurturing motherhood kept titillating my imagination, awakening the dormant sentiment in the recesses of my mind—indeed, the ultimate meaning encoded in human interaction with Mother Nature, the perennial font of poetic expression. By simply living on the Qinghai Plateau for a few brief seasons, as an eyewitness to the mighty rivers, the pristine lakes, the temple-like Kunlun mountain ranges, the eagles sailing across the skies, the tiny tents pitched on the grassland, the snow lotus flowers growing on a rock, and the frail figure of a Tibetan grandma gray with age, I can testify that they all make fit themes for poetry, which, I once declared, makes Qinghai a poetic plateau. It is precisely on account of this fact of that I went all out to launch the Qinghai Lake International Poetry Festival back in 2007 in the capacity of deputy provincial governor in charge of culture and education.

One can safely assume that the band of nomads who first roamed about before stumbling upon this landmass, were the first to raise their voice in token of thanksgiving, no matter how bleak and unforgiving it could be during certain hard and harsh periods of the year. As a rule, folk songs, ballads, and heroic epics have all been gems of poetic flowerings of our forebears in different parts of the globe. We all know that throughout most of the T'ang, the dynasty known for military expansion by the imperial

骚客的自觉创作，对这座高原的关注也由来已久。从汉王朝施行屯垦戍边以来，追随大潮的文人，便开始了对青海高原的书写，而作为历史与神话的源泉，人们对西羌之地、昆仑诸神的追溯更为久远。尤其是唐代，唐蕃之间发生一系列大事件，引发诗人们极大的热情。然而，纵观历史，青海作为边地和高原，人们记述更多的，除了山宗水源，便是战争与灾难，最令人记忆深刻的当属杜甫《兵车行》中的描述："君不见，青海头，古来白骨无人收。新鬼烦冤旧鬼哭，天阴雨湿声啾啾！"以及"青海城头空有月，黄沙碛里本无春""青海长云暗雪山"等这样的诗句。这当然只反映了一种特殊的历史背景。明清以及近代以来，随着高原的稳固与安定，诗人开始渐渐关注高原生活的温馨与自然的美好。清代杨应琚不仅兢兢业业治理河湟之地，也用诗篇表达对这片土地的

court over its extensive Western borders, poets of national eminence displayed a passion for the alpine landscape vastly different from that of China's interior, for the travails and tribulations experienced by the pioneers farming or stationed here as garrison soldiers, and for some kind of understanding with heavens or the mythical antiquity associated with the Kunlun deities. A large portion of the T'ang poetry is so concerned with the Tang-Tubot wars that there is a sense, the Chinese arch virtue for moderation and reticence notwithstanding, the T'ang poets too often broke out in lamentation against the desolation and devastation wrought by the incessant and protracted border hostilities. One easily detects a high-pitched note of sadness and bitterness, for instance, in Du Fu's "Song of the War-Carts":

Haven't you seen how

Bones from ancient times

Lie, bleached and unclaimed, scattered along the shores of Qinghai(Sky-blue Seas)

How the bitter weeping of old ghosts is

Joined by new voices, the gray sky by chittering rain.(David Hinton)

Or the famous poet anchored in the army camps, Wang Changling when he decries:

Clouds of Qinghai have darkened mountains clad in snow

Of course, among the poetic outpourings, we should find poetry of every kind, from fiery lambasting of war to exaltations of feelings, etc. As the highlanders settled down to more mundane rhythms of peace and stability, as in the cases of the Ming and Qing Dynasties, poetic production was in sync with the more sunny side of life on the plateau and the beauty of nature, replacing the images of the desolation and otherworldly splendor that arose from these far-flung territories. For instance, a Qing mandarin and poet, Yang Yingju, tells how he leads a battle against starvation instead of barbarians while overseeing the irrigation projects along the Huangshui River valley, a tributary of the Yellow River in the eastern Qinghai, for

热爱："溪外一群沙鸟白，麦中几片菜花黄"，清人张思宪也有诗赞道："湟流一带绕长川，河上垂杨拂翠烟。把钓人来春涨满，溶溶分润几多田？"其清新舒展，一改前人苍凉压抑的情调。

20 世纪 20 年代，以青海湖之名立省以来，"青海"一词便不限于一片湖水，而是涵盖了这广袤的高原大地。从 50 年代大规模的西部开发，到最近四十年的改革开放，青海以前所未有的形象进入诗人视野，青海湖国际诗歌节更是赢得了全世界诗人的热情关注和参与，中外诗人为这里抒写了大量美妙而优秀的诗篇，让这座诗的高原愈加熠熠生辉。

我无法一一评说这些杰出的诗篇，因为诗人们的创作涉及到青海的自然地理、历史人文、社会发展、人民生活、民间风情等各个方面。这些吟诵者包括卓有成就的老一代诗人，富有实力的中坚力量，充满创造力的青年才俊。

poverty could be a more merciless and savage enemy for the highland farming population than the terror of war:

I see a flock of white gulls on the sandbars over the creek,

And several strokes of rapeseed flowers in the wheat field.

Zhang Sixian, another Qing poet exhorts his fellow folks to enjoy "the sparse beauty of life" the plateau has to offer by sharpening their aesthetic sensibilities:

The Huangshui River encircles the flatlands like belt;

Willow trees hover over the water like emerald mist.

One spots anglers at times land on his catch

How many fields will be irrigated for autumn harvest?

So tenderly do poets take delight in the little things, lingering by the willows, feasting on the colors of rapeseed flowers, or as anglers who conspicuously "lie down" amid the grind of their daily chores.

Since the province was founded (named after the Qinghai Lake) during the Republican years in the 1920s, the word "Qinghai" has had a denotation not limited to the traditional outlying frontiers, and a connotation far beyond the graves amid the yellow sand dunes where the legionnaires conscripted to guard the forts of Qinghai, the large swathes of forbidding mountains, no-man's Gobi Desert and the like. Qinghai became a full administrative region of the PRC, which has since registered unprecedented social and economic development, followed by China's reform and opening up to the world per se in the late 1970s, it is therefore inevitable that the complexity and intricacy of the brave new world should enter into the purview of a new generation of Chinese poets. "Nothing is concealed. And a new civilization is revealed," especially in the wake of the inauguration of the Qinghai Lake International Poetry Festival in 2007, this plateau province has been drawing inquisitive and curious eyes from around the world. An invitation sent to party out here means more than just a pilgrimage, the memory of which will be cherished by the poet for the remainder of

他们从高原蕴藏的诗性中汲取营养、获得灵感，注入自己的知识、观察、感悟，面对这座触动身心的高原自然、人文与生活，调动想象力，突破固有的藩篱，重新探索文字的奥秘、把握语言的力量，创作了视野广阔、关注深入、题材丰富、风格多样的诗篇。

我不能一一评述这些诗篇。因为它们诞生于每个诗人富有个性的情怀。有人热衷于描写雪山，有人则偏爱雪山下的牧人；有人眺望青海湖的浩渺，有人则看见湖畔的一弯溪流；有人被森林草原所感动，有人则热爱一棵无名草、一株格桑花；有人震撼于贯穿高原的唐蕃古道，有人则迷恋一片残陶上的纹理；有人在这里穿越群山，有人则坐下来遥望星空；有人在大漠追逐落日的宏伟，有人则在河湟山村挽留炊烟的轻柔；有人探寻古城古刹的回声，有人则倾

his or her life. It is demonstrably the same landscape, the same people, but the poet, home and abroad, seems to exclaim—how delightful it is to watch the progress of the world! The sorrow and the tautness of the past is gone and in its place is a new alignment of forces, a more intimate understanding of suffering in history and in real time, a greater freedom of metrical arrangement as well as some measure of suggestiveness rendered more compelling.

I claim no authority to comment on these outstanding poems, as this collection represents but a tiny fraction of the treasures that all the budding talents and established poets alike having journeyed here, have written about this alpine province in their one-week long sojourn to attend the biennial poetic festival during their long pilgrimage of Chinese poetry at large. In deference to such poetic excellence out of my monumental ignorance, I must plead in attempt to achieve the impossible-a task that suggests the immensity lying behind this brief exploration of Chinese poets who have been humbled, standing in awe of the majestic beauty and humanistic riches this plateau province contains. Here are the poems—nay rather, here are the encomia—inspired by the land and its inhabitants, the jubilant emotions strongly felt, the sentiment of awe and humility made luminous. In sum, the range of work addresses a number of aspects of both human experience and natural process that strike poets as emblematic, revealing how it is lived by modern highlanders from a perspective typical of those from the interior provinces, which reinforces the perception that the plateau must count such a holy and hallowed spot deserving to be seen as Mecca for poets who need to streamline their poetics to create new possibilities and revitalize their skills as craftsmen in the evolving Chinese poetic tradition.

Again, I plead ignorance before these poetic gleanings. Each poet has his personality and develops his own style. One is enthralled at the foot of a snow-capped mountain, while another, agonized and worrying over dazzling pace of modernization in eastern China, finds solace in the way

听现代生活的旋律；有人陶醉于青稞酒的浓烈，有人则喜欢酥油茶的醇香；有人在史诗中穿越时空，有人则在牧歌中流连忘返；有人刻画老人脸上深邃的皱纹，有人则描摹少女眼中清澈的光彩；有人是阳光下的骑手，有人则是夜梦中的行者……

纵观数十年现代诗人歌咏青海的作品，我可以肯定地说，在高原的历史上，在这片神奇的地域上，青海，没有哪个时代像今天这样被诗人以如此的广度和深度关注过，更没有被诗人以如此规模和篇章书写过。这是我们这个时代诗人献给高原的礼物，是诗人们为对高原历史文化的卓越贡献。

这部诗集被冠以"歌咏青海的最美现代诗"，我觉得，编者之所以使用"最美"一词，那只是因为他们想要表达一种发自内心的敬仰，一种由衷的称赞之情。他

the herdsmen ply their ancient trade under the vast dome of the sky on their turf with their herds ; A considerable amount of poetic memories are imbued in the texture of things on the grassland, be they a pebble of Yellow River, a kite flying over the ancient town of Danger(Huangyuan), pottery shards reminiscent of the Neolithic Age, the sight of the rising sun glinting on the pastures. Cultural heroes, such as Wang Luobin, " the Folk Song King of Western China" and Chang Yao, the first highland poet who achieved national renown are fondly celebrated. Most poets recall a tour of the Kumbum Monastery a once-in-a-lifetime experience and believe they find consolation and salvation as they watch the Tibetan maid prostrates herself in front of the statue of Tsongkhapa, founder of the mainstream sect of Tibetan Buddhism. The vastness and majestic beauty of Qinghai Lake, of course, has been a recurring theme. "The imagery is swift, the pen races the thought, the heart beats time, the invention never falters." to quote Robert Payne in *Forever China*. But beneath and around all this is an ethos of tender piety, an enlightened euphoria over progress and bio-process, and last but not least, a sober reappraisal of past obsession with ego and possessions in an overtly consumerist age of ours.

Thumbing through these pieces, I am overwhelmed by a sense that this collection is in itself a miracle, as it constitutes a monument, unprecedented, unrivalled, to the beauty and bounty of the plateau as well as the humanity and piety of the highlanders. I can certainly vouchsafe this land of wonder has never been so poetically looked at, ruminated and written about. The land, the plateau, together with its awesome array of monasteries, its drove of pious-minded pilgrims, its torrential waterways of national importance, its epic grassland, is permanent. No poets can make it holier. The landscape, for all its bleakness and its periods of unforgiving climate, inspires poetry that is a sure sign of its spiritual strength.

Editors suggest to subtitle this anthology "the most beautiful modern poems about Qinghai". I trust epithets like "the most beautiful", although in superlative, amply convey the cultural shock experienced by

们和读者都知道，尚有许多优秀诗人、许多歌咏青海的美好诗篇未能收编，而更多最美的诗篇有待产生。

poets who trip from the interior to this land which used to be on the edge of traditionally cultural China. A most rewarding, eye-opening and fulfilling trip as most agree. The only regret as editors: they must choose amid so much excellence while wailing at more being left out for the project.

诗的高原
My Heart's
In The Highlands

歌咏青海的最美现代诗
100 Poems Dedicated to
the Poetic Plateau Called Qinghai

目

录

Contents

青海的草

傅天琳

蜿蜒不绝的被子，纯棉的，
弹性的
轻轻一按就会跳起来的
高原八月的另一层皮肤
是青海的草

经幡拂动下的吉祥文字，
生生不息的
牛的，羊的，马的，连虫子
都想生根发芽的
是青海的草

用情歌，酒，和生命源头的水
浇灌。醉人的，静谧而热烈的
让花儿一朵比一朵唱得嘹亮
是青海的草

在蜿蜒不绝的碧绿的早祷声中
让我埋下头去，朴素地嚼着
吟诵着。让我的蹄子点点点点
一步步靠近天堂
是青海的草

QINGHAI'S GRASSLAND

Fu Tianlin

A quilt of giant magnitude, cottony and elastic,
Bouncing back the minute you press it down,
Forming the highlands' fresh layer of skin in August—
This is Qinghai's grassland.

Where auspicious scriptures wave on the prayer flags
In an ever—blooming paradise of bovine, caprine and equine,
Where even the caterpillars take root as fungi—
This is Qinghai's grassland.

Irrigated by the headwaters of lyric, liquor and life,
Enchanting, soothing while still ecstasizing,
Turning the folk songs into outpourings of joy—
This is Qinghai's grassland.

Admist the green and blooming morning prayers
Let me bury my head, austerely munching and
Chanting. Make my clattering hooves
Approach Heaven step by step
Upon Qinghai's grassland.

青稞

北塔

有酒做媒
在来到青藏高原之前
我就与青稞结下了姻缘

世上哪还有另一种作物
在果实累累时
依然能青葱如此

少点氧气怕什么
青稞善于吸收更多别的养分
以更加持久的方式成长

只要有太阳的照应
无须暑气的考验
无须冰雪的锤炼
照样能走向成熟

在世界最高的高原
青稞拥有最多的沃土
却弯着腰低着头

我只是来一睹青稞的芳容
没想过要用镰刀迎娶她
收割的季节远未到来

她不会下嫁平原的我
但她会化身为酒
进入并占领我的灵魂

HIGHLAND BARLEY

Bei Ta

With wine as matchmaker,
I have tied the knot with highland barley
Long before I arrived on the highlands.

What other crop in the world
Can remain so lush and luxuriant
While dangling with fruit ?

What matters if oxygen be scarce—
This crop is good at absorbing other nutrients
To achieve everlasting growth.

So long as the sun is shining,
What need is there for summer's furnace
Or winter's freeze
Where it will grow full-fledged regardless ?

It is endowed with the most fertile soil
Upon the world's highest altitude,
Yet it bows its head in humility.

I have come here just for a glimpse of her,
Without ever fancying to marry her with my sickle,
Since it is far too early to harvest.

And she will not deign to marry me, a mere plain boy,
As she will be distilled into liquor,
Infiltrating and then taking the throne in my heart.

在青海湖畔

高瑛

看了一辈子云，
这儿的云最白；
望了一辈子的天，
这儿的天最蓝。

多想长出翅膀，
在空中飞翔，
揉揉闪亮的云，
摸摸透明的天。

再作一首诗，
写在高高的天壁上：
美丽的青海湖呵，
我爱你风光无限。

TRAIPSING ON THE SHORES OF QINGHAI LAKE

Gao Ying

I've been watching the clouds all my life.

The clouds here are the whitest, I reckon.

I've been gazing at the sky all my life.

The sky here is the bluest, I will testify.

How much I want to grow a pair of wings!

Taking to the sky.

Rubbing shoulders with the shining clouds.

Feeling the celestial transparency.

Writing a good poem.

Upon the high walls of the sky:

Beautiful Qinghai Lake.

You beauty has truly charmed me.

勒

古马

高高的草原上
云影铺开狼皮

你我面对面坐着
就像文成公主和松赞干布

鸟翅朝东。雪山向西
西天火烧云恍若布达拉宫

青海一碗酒
我用雄狮之血报答你的胭脂

背后羚羊飞奔
羚羊飞奔，一起奔向众妙之门

注：勒，青海湖流域藏族民间酒曲。

WINE SONG

Gu Ma

Over the grassland.

Clouds spread shadows like a colossal wolf skin.

You and I are sitting face to face.

Like Tang Princess Wencheng and Tibetan Prince Songzan Gambo.

Birds's wings face east. The snow-capped mountains face west.

The western sky is ablaze like the Potala Palace.

A bowl of wine in Qinghai.

I repay your rouge with the blood of the lion.

Behind us antelopes gallop.

Towards the Door of Wonder.

盛满鸡尾酒的玻璃杯子

洪烛

青海湖有一副我看不见的调色板
调试出雪山的白、云朵的白
调试出天空的蓝、湖水的蓝
调试出草的绿、树的绿……
即使同一种颜色也有差别的
调色比调酒还要细心
我饮下一杯纯粹由多重色彩
构成的鸡尾酒。眼睛醉了！
"彩虹升起，拿它来做吸管……"

更慷慨的，是它还漫山遍野
泼出油菜花的金黄，绝对24K的金黄
打造成戒指或项链都可以

青海湖有一只我看不见的手
忙着把调好的颜料涂抹在画布上
此刻，正显形为巴掌大的蝴蝶
去抚摸油菜花

QINGHAI LAKE'S COCKTAIL

Hong Zhu

Qinghai Lake has a palette invisible.

Coloring in white to debug snowed mountains and clouds.

Coloring out blue for the sky and the lake.

Green is made use of the grass and trees.

There are differences even in the same color.

Color mixing is an art subtler than wine blending.

I drink a glass made up of multiple colors.

A sort of cocktail . My eyes are drunk!

"The rainbow rises and uses it as a straw…"

A fairer and more generous scenery of the lakeside region.

Is sighted of the golden yellow of rapeseed fields, the absolute golden yellow of 24K.

That one can make into a ring or a necklace.

There is a hand I can't see in Qinghai Lake.

Mixing colors and toners on the canvas.

Incarnate of a butterfly the size of a palm.

To stroke the rapeseed flowers.

仰望雪山

胡的清

如同天才现世

雪山

总是出现在深蓝色背景里

让我仰望

把目光抬高

高出尘埃

把心举起来

放到教堂尖顶的位置

光

落到我脸上

以它的清冽拍打我——

这些来自恒河之外的微小的晶体

音乐般穿透我倦怠的肉体

直逼内心

仿佛无数苛责的眼

将最隐秘的黑暗洞穿

从俄堡到野牛沟

大巴在祁连山的褶皱里颠簸

车窗外不期而遇的雪山

以通体透明的存在

一再将我提醒

发出邀约

逼迫我抑制生理上的不适

对崇高与纯粹保持虔敬

对人性的弱点感到羞愧

并为自己所曾犯过

不曾犯过的罪行

深深忏悔

在海拔四千多米高地

仰望雪山

深蓝色天空

是一副巨大的镇静剂

以包容万有的沉寂

抚慰我缺氧的灵魂

A SNAPSHOT OF THE SNOW-CAPPED MOUNTAIN

Hu Deqing

Like a genius emerging in this world.

Snow Mountains.

Always loom against a dark blue firmament.

Let me look up.

Raise my eyes.

Above the dust.

Hoist my heart.

Atop the church spire.

Light

Falls on my face.

Beat me with its clearness—

These tiny crystals from outside the Ganges.

Music penetrates my weary body.

Goes straight to the heart.

Like countless critical eyes.

See through the most secret darkness.

From Oborg to Buffalo Valley.

Our bus bumped in the folds of the snow-capped Qilian Mountains.

One peak after another mountain outside the window.

Whose transparent presence.

A constant prompter.

A constant invitation extended to me.

Forcing me to restrain my physical discomfort.

Humbling me before the throne of the sublime and the pure.

Aware of the weakness of human nature.

Repenting

For a crime that has never been committed.

Profound repentance.

At an altitude of more than 4,000 meters above sea level.

Looking up at the snow-capped mountains.

Dark blue skies.

What a powerful tranquilizer.

That contains a mountain of silence.

Soothing my anoxic soul.

青海

姚风

在我生活的欲望之城
我就是我的笼子

里面囚禁的，是我自己
狱卒，也是我自己

在青海，我要打开笼子
把自己放出来

我要放出群山
放出江河，放出草原

我还要放出蓝天
多么嘹亮的蓝天啊

青海，我要为你写一首诗
但不会把你比作天堂

QINGHAI

Yao Feng

In the city of desires where I live.
I serve my own cage.

It is myself who is imprisoned inside.
The jailer, it's me, too.

In Qinghai, I want to open the cage.
Let myself out.

I'm going to release the mountains, too.
Release the rivers, the grasslands.

There is still the blue sky to be freed.
What a mighty blue sky!

Qinghai, I'm going to write a poem for you.
But I am still reticent enough to call you Paradise.

为一种蓝命名

靳晓静

在日益丰盈的秋天里
端坐如神
为远方的蓝命名
命名，原本是上帝的本分和荣光

在秋天，为一种蓝命名是困难的
况且它是水，摇晃不定

说它是藏地天空的蓝吧
它更深一点，并且以鳃呼吸
说它是极地大海的蓝
它更静一点，静到用经幡说话

它比蓝宝石的蓝
多了些许柔软的部分
它比船长夫人眼中的蓝
多了一份不来不去的安稳

它是望一眼就让人静穆的蓝
是我们皮肤下隐隐可见的蓝
是止住世上一切喧嚣的蓝

夺命的蓝，爱情的蓝
它只能是青海湖的蓝

PONDER A KIND OF BLUE

Jin Xiaojing

In the increasingly abundant autumn.

Reigning supreme like God.

Who names the color in the distance blue.

The divine grace and duty.

It is difficult to ascertain the arch color of an alpine autumn.

I mean the massive body of water of Qinghai Lake.

Blue of the typical Tibetan sky.

It's a little deeper, breathing through its gills.

Or the blue of the polar sea ?

But it's quieter, quieter enough to speak with prayer flags.

It's bluer than sapphire.

But soft−tinted.

Bluer than what comes into the eyes of the captain's wife on a sea−faring ship.

There is an extra security that can't come or go.

It is a blue that tranquilizes at a glance.

The faint blue under our blood veins.

The ultimate brakes to stall all the hustle and bustle in the world.

The blue of life, the blue of love.

The crown color only worthy of Qinghai Lake.

在互助土司府邸听花儿

柯平

暮色低压着檐角
木笛裂处，泉水呜咽
金子的骨头、珠饰的泪点
帷幔背后，铰链拖动时光

如同麦穗在铁器下啜泣
最初的颤音里，牦牛垂首
彩陶也袒露古老的伤口
落日如磨盘，压弯多少脊背
花儿与少年，中间是无尽的沧桑

歌声又顺着经幡逆风而上
在高处盘绕，战栗
然后从鹰的健翅迅速滑落
偶尔的寂静里
藏有多少雷霆
雪垛、草原、寺庙
木轮车的直轴，碾过沉沉长夜

HEARING FOLK SONGS PERFORMED
AT THE CHIEFTAIN HOUSE IN HUZHU COUNTY

Ke Ping

The gloaming weighs heavily on the eave's four corners;
A spring gushes out through the cracks on a wooden flute.
The gold-rimmed skulls tells a tale with its beaded tears.
Twisting the curtain winch unleashes a tumultuous current of time,

Crying out like wheat heads weeping under the snatching iron tools,
In melodious trills dating back to time immemorial, when yaks listlessly drooped their heads,
And painted pottery gaped naked, parading their ancient wounds.
The rotund sunset, like the weight of a grindstone, made too many backs crooked.
Song of My Youth has camouflaged too much untold suffering under its florid lyrics.

The songs follow the flutter of the prayer flags, soaring against the wind,
Hovering on high, awe-inspiring trepidations,
Then falling fast like the agile wings of an eagle.
Just how much explosive force is hidden
In the transitory stillness.

Snow-clad haystacks. The grassland. A monastery.
The rodlike axle of a wooden cart grinds over the benighted field.

我的阿丽玛、格桑花

我的青稞酒、酥油茶

我的互助令的老爷山

和大眼睛的青海湖

上去高山望平川哪

皮囊与盐巴下面，生活在延续

下四川的哥哥回来

风霜满面，背着神像低语

在黑暗中收集火焰与祈盼

并在羊皮卷上镌刻下来

最后的音节是雪峰崩塌

和马蹄疾驰发出的那一阵轰响

我知道，这动情的声音

来自舞台上歌者哽咽的嗓眼

也来自文化强悍的内心

My fair lady— My Sims Azalea—

My highland barley spirits— My yak butter tea—

My Old Man Mountain of Huzhu County—

And my big gaping Qinghai Lake...

You climb a mountain to look at the whole prairies.

Inside a sack of skin, life goes on along with lake salt.

Older Brother returns from the Szechwan lowlands,

Wearing wind and frost on his face, muttering, his back

turned against the religious statue...

You gathered flames and hopes from the dark,

Transcribing them onto parchment rolls.

The last syllable let loose an avalanche from the snow summit

And the rumbling of coursers' hooves.

The moving voice, I knew came from

The sobbing throat of the singer on the stage,

As well as the stout, sturdy heart of a stalwart civilization.

高原上的海

寇宗鄂

在湖泊的家族中
你独有海的血统
高原从你开始
有了带咸味儿的风景
雪线上的春天
是一幅江南绣锦
翠绿里镶着嫩黄，是你
夏天的热情
湛蓝与辽阔，是你
接纳与包容的本真
每滴水的诱惑
都富含生命的养分
于是，你的温馨
成为湟鱼的家园
成为候鸟的天堂
人间的梦境
我是一只迟到的候鸟
心驰神往了大半生

THE SEA ON THE PLATEAU

Kou Zonge

In the family of lakes.

You boast a unique pedigree.

Of all plateaus, you are the beginning.

A landscape smacking of salt.

Spring on the snow line.

Redolent of the lush rice paddies down stream of the Yangtze

Bright yellow in the green.

The warmth of summer enthusiasm.

Blue and vast, it's you.

The truth of acceptance and tolerance.

The temptation of every drop of water.

Rich in the nutrients of life.

Therefore, your warmth, bounty, zest.

Turns into the home to a special breed of fish－Qinghai Carp.

A paradise for migratory birds.

The Dream of the World.

I count myself, for one, among the migratory birds.

Though late, my dream has at last come true.

格桑花

蓝蓝

八个瓣的石头，会飞的石头
我秘密的爱认出了你。

啊，红色的炭块，白色的火焰
燃烧在八月的高原。

你是穷人的前额，风的情人
你是一个人的童年深藏在他泪水的晶莹中。

我从你对高原的忠诚里
分得了幸福的允诺和低垂的羞赧。

恍惚间我记起另一个八月
是谁曾用指着你的手把我点燃?

格桑花，你用最小的闪电把我抓住
——由于你
那往昔一刻不停地走到今天……

SIMS AZALEA FLOWERS

Lan Lan

A stone with eight petals, a stone that can fly.
My secret love finds you.

Ah, red charcoal, white flame.
Burning on the plateau in August.

You are the forehead of the poor, the
lover of the wind.
You are a person's childhood hidden in
the crystal of his tears.

From your loyalty to the plateau.
I have had my share of the promise of
happiness and the drooping shyness.

In a trance, I recall another August.
Who sets me on fire with the hand
pointing at you ?

Sims azalea, you caught me off guard with
the smallest lightning.
Because of you.
I have followed some clues in search of
you to this day.

恩泽

老乡

上游的羊　没有喝饱
牛　没能饮足——
河的下游　还有众多
干渴的朋友

江河源头的雪山
已经很瘦很弱了
在她挤出的奶水里
现已布满晚霞的血丝
但她的乳汁　依然在滴

"上善若水　厚德载物"
谁能载动上游
对下游的殷殷关爱
谁就能　出了青海
代表青海

GRACE

Lao Xiang

The sheep upstream are not feeding well.

The cow do not drink enough—

More herd in the lower reaches of the river;

Are still thirsty.

Snow lines are retreating fast,

At the source of rivers.

In the milk squeezed out;

It is mixed with the blood of the sunset.

But her milk is still dripping.

The greatest benevolence is like water;

The highest good contains and nourishes all.

What about those sentient beings upstream？

And those downstream.

One who benefits all;

Deserves in behalf of Qinghai.

翅翼信赖的沃土

李松涛

日月山上空的日月，挥拨迷雾，
居高临下，指出：
社会与大自然的双边关系，
急需重塑！

人哪，并非有意逗留于往昔，
实在没有突围之路。
肆意妄为，导致险境危途！
上帝用深奥的目光，
看人类惯性地滑向坟墓。

我们与大自然的万物，
都沾亲带故——
人类从这个认识上开始成熟。

为一朵祥云注册，
给一阵清风签证，
对一片绿叶实施监护。

啄木鸟的翅翼像句眉批，
写在疏星朗月的空白处。

啊！仅剩的鸟儿衔仅剩的树种，
在雨云下飞舞，
于青海湖畔，找到了
一块值得翅翼信赖的沃土……

THE FERTILE SOIL UNDER THE CARE OF WINGS

Li Songtao

The sun and the moon above the Sun and Moon
Mountain, waving away the fog.
Condescendingly pointing out:
The bilateral relationship between man and nature,
Are badly in need of being remolded!

 I didn't mean to refuse to let the past bury its dead.
Man is, after all, a species prone to errors.
Wanton actions occasion complications which lead to
a dangerous road!
God sits motionless, with esoteric looks;
As the human world unstoppably gets worse.

Nature as impacted by humans;
Hangs on the thin line of human actions—
Thus signals human awakening.

He sets out to register for an auspicious cloud.
Issues visa to a breeze.
Brings a green leaf into protection.

The wings of a woodpecker are like eyebrows.
Written in the space of the sparse stars and the
moon.

Ah! The only remaining birds are carrying the
seeds of the only remaining tree species.
Flying across the rain clouds.
On the banks of Qinghai Lake, I find them.
A piece of fertile soil worthy of trust on the part
of wings.

跟着一只蝴蝶飞翔

李琦

在青海
我颈上的银蝴蝶
忽然就不见了
失落　无奈
因为有太多美好绵长的回忆
在那蝴蝶之上

诗人树才说
那个拾到蝴蝶的　也许是个小姑娘
想想看　她会多喜欢呵
这样说的时候　他的声音动人
他大眼睛的妻子在他身旁
深深地点了一下头

我的朋友多好
手指轻轻一抬
就让迷茫之人
看到了另外的方向

起风了
风吹油菜花明黄的丝绒
风吹青海湖湛蓝的绸缎
这么好的风

也一定在吹拂一个目光清澈的女孩
她辫发黝黑　面颊绯红
颈上忽然飞来的一只蝴蝶
正闪动银质的光芒

小小蝴蝶　机缘玄妙
通灵一样　它找到了一个
正在渴望飞翔的人
一切相得益彰
少女的心事　纯银的翅膀

我还想　把我佩戴时曾有过的愉悦
把一个经历沧桑之人的祝福
一并送给　那个女孩
多好　素不相识　从东北到西北
我们两代女人
跟着一只蝴蝶飞翔

FLY WITH A BUTTERFLY

Li Qi

In Qinghai.

The silver butterfly alighting on my neck.

Suddenly flies off.

I am lost and helpless.

As so many beautiful and long memories.

Evaporate with her.

Poet Shucai said.

Catching butterflies is a favorite pastime with young girls.

A patent weakness.

In a voice moving and convincing.

His wife with big eyes beside him;

Nodded in agreement.

What a wise friend!

Whose counsels clenched an argument once and for all.

The confused saw better.

As his fingers showed the direction.

The wind arose.

Blown across the bright yellow velvet of rapeseed fields.

Over the blue satin of Qinghai Lake.

A nice wind it was.

Must be blowing a girl with sparkling eyes.

Her braided hair was dark and her cheeks were flushed.

A butterfly suddenly flew around her neck.

Flashing silver light.

Karma it must be about the little butterfly.

So elusive like a spirit, a vision.

About someone who happens to be in the mood to fly.

Beautiful coincidence.

The thoughts of a maiden, the wings of sterling silver.

I also want to pass along the pleasure I once had.

Together with the blessing of a person who has known human joys and sorrows.

To that girl.

Both strangers, one from the northeast (which is me) and her, a local in the northwest.

Two generations of women.

Fly with a butterfly.

遥远的青海湖

俸伍拉且

对于我来说，青海湖极其遥远
远在天边
远在地角
远在我的现实生活之外

蓝蓝的水
咸咸的水
与我的现实天空一样蓝蓝的水
与我的汗水血液一样咸咸的水

所以，青海湖对于我来说
属于梦境
属于梦境世界
属于梦境世界里的水

所以我去了青海湖
乘飞机去，从大凉山迎着太阳出发
迎着太阳到达
太阳照耀我的角度几乎没有变化

常言道人往高处走
水往低处流
这样一湖蓝蓝的水咸咸的水
却在最高处荡漾

就这样，我完成了一个愿望
让青海湖，遥远的青海湖
在我和我的大凉山身旁
碧波荡漾

因为在高处，在高高的地方
所以青海湖高高在上
青海湖的水因此而纯洁
因此而高贵因此而神圣

当我希望现实生活的水
都往高处流的时候
梦境也就成了现实
现实也就成了梦境

当然还有许多许多原因
比如青海湖边一尘不染的眼睛
人的眼睛
牛羊的眼睛

对于我来说
遥远的青海湖不再遥远
遥远的只是我和我的大凉山
与青海湖之间的物理的距离

比如牵着鹰翅飞行的
挽着清风飘扬的
神圣的诗词
高贵的歌唱

THE QINGHAI LAKE IS FAR-AWAY

Luowu Laqie

The Qinghai Lake is far-away in my head,

Far-away by the horizon,

Where the land meets the sky,

Far, far beyond my quotidian sight.

So in a sense, the Qinghai Lake lives only in my head,

In my dream spectacles,

Mirages of my dreamland,

A dreamland that must be a watery kingdom.

They say very often that, as men aspire to fly high,

So waters humbly runs down—

Yet somehow this pure gem of brinish blue is really

Brimming upon the highland of highlands in glee.

And high it is, up on the highlands,

The Qinghai Lake looking over all under heaven.

And hence its sublime purity,

And hence its noble sacredness.

Yet this has many other causes too, like

The pristine eyes by the lakeside

Of the people,

Of those grazing the pastureland,

Like that which inspires the eagles' determined flight,

And the breeze's meandering breath:

The holy utterance of a poet

Chanting a psalm to his heart's content.

Water so blue,

Water so brinish—

Blue as the broad daylight;

Brinish as the sweat and the blood of my body.

So I went—

So I went to the Qinghai Lake by plane,

Sailing atop the sun rising from my home mountains,

Shining upon me at almost a fixed angle.

In the meantime, the Qinghai Lake,

Blue and blooming, distant in the highlands,

Was right by me and my mountains' side,

And so my long-time dream came true.

When I wish the water of people's life

All to flow upwards instead of down,

It happens that dream and reality

Will exchange their proper places.

So to me, the Qinghai Lake

No longer is far-away.

What is far-away, though, is the physical distance

Between it and me, and my mountains where the sun rises.

鄂陵湖与扎陵湖

马新朝

1

很多人在奔跑
它们排成队，消失又重生
每个人都怀抱着寒冷
守护着湖水中的高度

2

那个坐在湖中心的老人
身穿黑大氅，白嘴鸥向远处运送着
坚定与沉默，它手拽白云
把蓝天与湖水缝制在一起

3

湖，把它藏在水中的严厉
从西风中拿出来，放在
一架白色的牛骨上
黑鹰在细读

4

三百公里之外
废墟东边，一尾牧草用细茎举着绿
那是湖的话
说给远处的藏包听

5

灯亮了
那是谁的家啊，女人们躲在厨房里
忙碌、唠叨，闪亮的银饰
在湖水上荡开

ELING LAKE AND ZHALING LAKE

Ma Xinchao

1

A group of people are running.

In a line—up, now are here and then gone.

Everyone is holding the cold in his breast.

Guarding the height of the lake.

2

An old man sitting in the middle of the lake.

Dressed in black, white—headed gulls are transported into the distance.

Firm and silent, in forging an alliance;

He has sewn the blue sky with the lake.

3

The lake, showing its gruesome face,

Against the harsh west wind.

The white skull of a yak,

Induces a Black Hawk to read carefully.

4

Three hundred kilometers away.

To the east of the ruins, a forage grass grows.

The language of the lake.

The message intended for the white felt yurts in the distance.

5

The light is on.

Whose yurt is that ? The Tibetan housewife is cooking.

Busy, nagging, shiny silver ornaments.

Swinging on the lake.

柳湾：陶的歌声

吕霞

青海之东，湟水逶迤
陶的碎片编拼神秘音符
在河流的波纹间飘扬
梦呓和哭泣的姿势
已不能辨认
谁的梦如此纷乱
谁的哭泣如此伤悲

双耳的陶聆听着久远的记忆
泥土的脚步
在陶的年轮中浮现
故事没有始终

卷唇的陶诉说着
陶前凝望的眸子
水的倩影和泪珠交叠
铜镜里第一根白发
光芒如炽

流泪的手，握不住分离的消息
陶啊，柳湾的河流间齐声歌唱的陶
湮没了往昔的马蹄声
梦中的心事不曾消解

蛙纹的密码迈着
优雅的舞步
历史的队伍里孰先孰后

信仰与巫术携手演绎
悲情是跳跃变形的符号
叙述最初的秘密

滞留在幸存的语境里
聆听、诉说，然后歌唱
把久远的记忆传递到
更为久远的时刻

THE SINGING OF POTTERY IN LIUWAN

Lv Xia

To the east of Qinghai, the Huangshui River meanders east.

Pottery fragments scattered weave mysterious notes.

Making music upon the rippling water.

The postures of somniloquy or weeping ?

Nobody can tell.

Who dreams so ominously ?

Who weeps so vehemently ?

One piece of pottery with two ears listens to the distant memory.

The footsteps of the earth.

Emerge in the rings of pottery.

A tale that has no beginning or end.

Another item, with her lips curled, narrates.

Her gazing eyes.

The beautiful shadow of the water overlaps with tears.

The first white hair in the bronze mirror.

Shines ablaze.

A tearful hand can't hold the news of separation.

Pottery, singing in unison along the rivers in Liuwan.

Obliterates the sound of horses' hoofs of the past.

The worries in the dream have never been dispelled.

The code of the frog pattern is dancing.

Elegant dance steps.

Which comes at last to history.

Belief and witchcraft perform hand in hand.

Sadness is the dominant note.

The key clue to her esoteric beginning.

Stranded in the context of survival.

These remnant items of pottery are listening, speaking, and then singing.

And passing on murky memories to us.

Of a more murky moment.

青海湖的青

树才

青海湖的青，是青海的
青，是青天的青，
也是青出于蓝的青——

那青，几乎是透明的蓝，
几乎是湖水本身，
几乎比天空还空。

从那青里诞生了
青海！站在湖边——
你越看，天就越近。

那青，离天很近。
那青，离空也很近。
据说，天是空的。

什么能比青更青呢？
什么又是最青的青呢？
塔尔寺的钟声响了——

一双双手，高举过
头顶，然后是奋不顾身地
一拜，再拜：肉身没了……

但是……要慢慢来。
在高原，一切都要慢——
说话，走路，呼吸……

要慢慢接近青海湖的青。
别急，也不要奔跑，
否则你会憋得脸色发青。

青海湖的青肯定是唯一的。
藏在水里的盐可以证明，
开满岸边的油菜花也可以。

THE BLUE OF QINGHAI LAKE

Shu Cai

The blue of Qinghai Lake is customized.
Blue is the blue of the highland sky
Bluer than the blue itself.

That blue, almost transparent.
A lakeful of blue
Yet emptier than the sky.

Born from that blue.
Was the province named after the blue lake
The more you gaze, the nearer the sky
looms overhead.

The blue seems so close to the sky.
So close to the air.
The sky is likened to Void.

Is there anything bluer than the blue lake ?
What is the bluest ?
Ah, the bells of Ta'er Monastery ring out—

The pious pilgrim, prostrating himself.
A pair of hands, held high.
Atop of the head, and then devoutly.
One prayer after another, until his physical body is
gone.

But. Take your time.
On the plateau, everything is getting slow—
To talk, to walk, to breathe...

It is necessary to slowly approach the shores of
Qinghai Lake.
Don't worry, don't run.
Or you'll turn blue.

The blue of Qinghai Lake must be unique.
Such as the salt hidden in the lake waters can attest.
As well as the rapeseed flowers in full blossom.

女湖之美

梅卓

她是美的。当四季轮转
绿雨到白雪
飘向女神的黛眉青眸
她早已看断世间百态
仍愿意红颜不变
犹如浓烈的一声惊叹
悬挂在大地的心脏
草尖上的风已经吹走千年
湖泊上的花朵依然灿烂

她是美的。当传说蔓延
时光和空间
容纳高僧大德的颂词
也容纳了凡夫俗子的祈祷
她欲言又止
却从没有停下繁衍的脚步
她的美丽如此有力
并非沉默的高原未曾诉说

创世前的第一道彩虹
漂染过她的松石
宇宙间的第一道闪电
装点在她的珠冠
还有第一个秘密
尚鲠在她的胸间
还有第一句歌谣
曾透露她的忧伤……

留下大自然的馈赠：
一个节日——
关于美
关于看到美时
眼睑上方突然而来的压力
那是承袭了怀旧的液体
是呈献给节日的贡品
晶莹剔透　毫无杂念
清洁一如湖水
呈献、呈献——
为她盛大之美
也为自己

THE BEAUTY OF A FEMALE LAKE

Mei Zhuo

She is beautiful. When the seasons rotate.

From spring rain to winter snow.

Alighting upon the goddess's eyebrows and green

eyes.

She has long seen everything in the world.

Still willing to remain the same.

Like a strong marvel.

Hanging in the heart of the earth.

The wind on the tip of the grass has blown away

for a thousand years.

The flowers on the lake are still brilliant.

She is beautiful. When legends spread.

Time and space.

Eulogies containing the great virtues of eminent

monks.

It also contains the prayers of ordinary people.

She hesitated to speak.

But never stopped the pace of reproduction.

Her beauty is so powerful.

It is not that the silent plateau has not spoken.

The first rainbow before the creation of the

world.

Bleached and dyed her pine stone.

The first bolt of lightning in the universe.

The makeup is on her beaded crown.

And the first secret.

Stuck in her chest.

And the first ballad.

Once revealed her sadness...

Leave behind the gift of nature:

A holiday—

About beauty.

About seeing beauty.

Sudden pressure above the eyelids.

It's a nostalgic liquid.

It's a tribute to the festival.

Glittering and translucent without

distractions.

Clean as a lake.

Present, present—

For her magnificent beauty.

And for yourself.

天堂，镜子

潇潇

今天的心情零下 30 度
风很大，日月山与青藏高原
在虚掩的词语上
呼吸急促

似乎难以想象
麻木与肉体开始结谋
夜晚打着喷嚏
像一个服苦役的病人

难以想象，青海湖
取下天堂的镜子
把一炉纯蓝的火苗
统统倒进了青海湖底

一湖燃烧的颜色啊
静静的，温文尔雅的暴力
零下 30 度，绝对的蓝色
多么干净，多么惊心动魄

仅仅一滴蓝
就把我要命的诗歌
从高处忧郁的湖底，分离了出来

仅仅一滴蓝
就大于高空的思想
大于气候中一个女人的命运

PARADISE,MIRROR

Xiao xiao

Today's mood is 30 degrees below zero.

The wind is howling, the Sun and the Moon

Mountain and the Qinghai−Tibet Plateau.

Upon the falsity of written words.

Barely out of breath.

It seems hard to imagine.

Numbness and the body begin to collude.

Sneezing at night.

Like a convert in a labor camp.

It's hard to imagine, Qinghai Lake.

Seizing the mirror of heaven.

Putting a furnace of pure blue fire.

Pouring them into the bottom of Qinghai Lake.

The burning color of a lake.

Quiet, gentle violence.

Minus 30 degrees, absolutely blue.

How clean, how thrilling.

One drop of blue alone.

Is enough to separate my fatal poem.

From the melancholic bottom of the lake.

Just a drop of blue.

Is greater than the idea of being high in the air.

Greater than the fate of a woman in the climate.

活在西宁

曲有源

我睡醒了一看
黄河还在
身边
历
史
也没有走远
能在西宁活着
不能不安宁
日子不用
愁了
只
要
从
几
千
年
前
扯过来
一根抻面
就能养活今天

A BRIEF SOJOURN IN XINING—ONE TRULY OFFBEAT EXPERIENCE

Qu Youyuan

I wake up and take a look.

The Yellow River is still there.

Around.

Calendar.

History.

It does not go far.

To be alive in Xining.

One cannot but slow down.

The gentle pace of living.

Gastronomes

Can

Have

A

Toe

Hold

On

Life

By savoring

The local specialty—

Noodles with beef meat.

青黄（仿河湟野曲"花儿"）

杨克

青海湖青　油菜花黄
黑白牦牛趟在那青黄缎缎儿上
尕妹子花儿一亮嗓
草原宽哎　长江长

月影子里下雪哩
那是羊毛毛在银剪下飘扬
少年的脸蛋儿灿灿亮
一线线阳光哎　洒在青稞上

大石头眼里的清泉水
风吹来时水动弹
青湛湛的沟沿上看谁呀
一对儿大眼睛的小姊妹

大黄风它把云刮散哪
一条黄河水滟滟
昆仑玉嫩得像青菜
一指头弹出一汪清水来

你看那几片早起的云朵
一眨眼就翻过了昆仑山
青海的湖水哟
记得一定把哥哥的思念捎上

THE BLUE OF QINGHAI LAKE THE GOLDEN YELLOW OF RAPESEED FIELDS(modeling the pattern of Hua'er, folk song popular in the irrigated area of Huangshui River)

Yang Ke

The Blue of Qinghai Lake. The Golden Yellow of Rapeseed Fields.

Yak, black and white, graze leisurely on the grassland.

A beautiful girl raises her voice.

In praise of the grassland and the Yangtze River flowing by.

Does it snow in the moon's shadow ?

Nothing but an illusion. It is wool sheared off on the ground.

The face of the lad is sunny.

A glimmer of sunshine is sprinkled on the Tibetan barley.

Crystal water, gushing out of a spring of a stone.

The water tremble as the wind blows over.

Who is out there peeping across the ditch ?

A big-eyed girl is coming along.

A gust of wind drive the clouds away.

The Yellow River flows east.

Kunlun jade is as tender as fresh vegetables.

Touched with a finger,water seeps out.

Look up at the clouds.

Crossing the Kunlun Mountains in the blink of an eye.

The lake waters in Qinghai.

Remember me to my love.

柳湾彩陶博物馆

杨宗泽

走进这座陶罐式建筑
等于走进一个梦
这个梦发源于遥远的上古
一直流淌到
电脑和数码相机控制下的今天

走进这座陶罐式建筑
就是走进一个梦
走进一个曾经喧闹千载的梦
一个已经沉寂百年的梦
一个正在春风杨柳般复苏的梦
这个梦是彩色的

走进这座建筑的时候
我觉得如同走进一个梦
而走出这座建筑
我怎么再也走不出那个梦

RAMBLING THOUGHTS IN LIUWAN
PAINTED POTTERY MUSEUM

Yang Zongze

I walk into this pot—shaped pottery museum.

As if roaming into the bucolic heart of Qinghai.

Traceable to bygone days.

Times immemorial.

Down to the present of computers and digital cameras.

I walk into this pot—shaped pottery museum.

As if into a dreamland.

Hot and noisy for thousands of years.

A dreamland that has been silent for a hundred years.

But becoming mute for the last couple of hundred years.

It has revived now like a willow in the spring breeze.

Full of color and motion.

I walk into this pot—shaped pottery museum.

As if into a dreamland.

As I step out of the facility,

My heart remains there.

神性的油菜花

桑恒昌

你见过黄金吗
你见过摇曳的黄金吗
你见过汹涌的黄金吗
你见过活的黄金吗
你见过散发芳香的黄金吗
你见过一座又一座
露天的黄金矿吗

贫瘠是它的营养
高寒是它的水分
吞着寂寞长大
吃着稀薄的空气开花

点亮大片大片的荒原
点亮大片大片的天空
也点亮大片大片的我们
青海湖张开大大的镜头
为我们和油菜花合影

采它的金黄
酿造精神
采它的黄金
熔炼灵魂

THE DIVINE RAPESEED FLOWERS

Sang Hengchang

Have you ever seen gold？

Have you ever seen flickering gold？

Have you ever seen surging gold？

Have you ever seen live gold？

Have you ever seen fragrant gold？

Have you ever seen gold mines,

You've seen one after another.In succession, in the
open？

These flowers literally and metaphorically feed on air.

Second, moisture.

Third, loneliness.

It does blossom miraculously.

Ignite the vast expanse of wilderness.

Light up the immense celestial vaults.

And huge crowds of human beings.

Qinghai Lake, equipped with extra−wide angle lens,

Takes a picture for us in the rapeseed fields.

Extract gold from them.

To brew a spirit.

Extract gold from rapeseed flowers.

To fortify our souls.

在青海

郁葱

在九月，我在同一个早晨，

见到了雪，阳光，雾和雨——这是青海。

在九月，我在同一个早晨，

见到了羊、牛、草和云，

见到了真正纯粹的人——这是青海。

青海有那么多的颜色，

可让人觉得，世界上其实只有一种颜色，

如果有一天，人找不到最终的归宿，那么你来青海。

如果有一天，植物再也找不到最初的种子，

——充满活性和爱的种子，那么你来青海。

我有足够的幸运，

知道了这个世界上，

依然还有真正的纯洁和圣洁，

有神灵、有神性，

有几乎能够想象的曼妙的一切。

也就是在那个九月，

我看到了因为爱和月亮而活着的女人——青海。

因为太阳和血性而活着的男人——青海。

苍穹老了，而青海年轻！

IN A MORNING IN SEPTEMBER

Yu Cong

In a morning in September,

I feast on mouth—watering panorama and idyllic grassland landscape

Snow, sunshine, fog and rain come and go—this is Qinghai.

In a morning in September,

Sheep, cattle, grass and clouds come in sight.

And real people with hearts of gold en route— this is Qinghai.

This land called Qinghai is full of colors.

Yet there is one color that is unique in the world.

If one day, anyone driven to desperate choices, try your luck in Qinghai.

If one day, we fail to find seeds for a special type of plants.

Try to retrieve them in Qinghai.

I'm lucky enough.

I know that in this world,

There is still purity and holiness.

Divinity and spirit.

Almost everything that can be imagined can be retrieved here.

It all happens in September.

Women, who live to love life and the moon in Qinghai.

Men who are full of sunshine and vitality in Qinghai.

The sky is old, but Qinghai is young!

藏地安多

班果

如果众水需要证明自己的血缘
那源头闪亮的脐带在指认你
在雪域　在高处的产床
你配享母亲生产的荣光　配享
儿女们呈献的蓝色哈达

如果群山重新寻找失落的族谱
那些闪光的男性名号：
阿尼玛卿、巴颜喀拉和年保玉则
一组父亲的姓氏重塑了雪峰
你有权以王者的名义分配天空和四季

如果黄金询问来路　白银打听去处
褐色的盆地，它紧闭的嘴唇在启示
如果飞禽祈求庇佑　鱼类恳请安居
蓝色的圣湖，你纯洁的双眸正好接纳

如果心在寻找归宿　灵魂
还在跋涉中渴求方向
安多的古寺　你的大殿宜于休憩
你长案上供奉的长明灯
适合指引，并且超度

TIBETAN AMDO

Ban Guo

If all the water bodies must prove their pedigree,

The hard evidence available, beyond doubt, is the headwater region.

brought into protection, the shining umbilical cord.

The maternity ward in the snowland.

Worthy of honor and glory attributed to maternity.

Deserving of all the Hada presented by her sons and daughters.

Suppose the mountains must ascertain their lost genealogy.

Those shiny male names:

Mount Amne Chen, Mount Bayan Kara and Mount Nianbao Yuze.

A list of father's surnames reshape all snow−capped mountains in Qinghai.

In the divine right of assigning duty to the sky and the four seasons.

If gold desires to know whence it comes, and silver, whither it goes.

The brownish basins close their lips in revelation.

If the birds and fish pray for blessings.

All the blue holy lakes are ready to give audience.

If the heart is looking for its home−the soul.

Still trudging for the right way.

All the monasteries in Amdo open to cater to your need.

The everlasting lamps.

Are sure to enlighten all the craving and spiritually hungry.

幻影

高兴

坎布拉，晴朗得如此暧昧，性感
手在抚摩，乳房却是透明的
远处的山忽然近了，贴着你的鼻子
漫步和拥抱的寂静。什么声音在响
什么词语在奔突

树林战栗。风竖起耳朵，吹过湖面
打探时间的消息
岸边，牧民赶着羊群，加快了步伐

那只鸟，再次飞临，停在船头
望了望我，又跃上顶棚。它多么自由
扑扇着羽翼，在蓝天下闪烁
仿佛公开的情敌，剥去女人的衣衫
故意刺激我，羞辱我，让我满脸通红
恨不得立即在光中死去

坎布拉，深秋，金黄的叶子正一片片飘落

VISION

Gao Xing

Kanbula, so sunny, so ambiguous, so sexy.

The hands are stroking, but the breasts are transparent.

The mountains in the distance appear suddenly near, close to your nose.

The silence of walking and hugging. What's that noise ?

What words are rushing along ?

The woods shudder. The wind pricks up its ears and blows across the reservoir.

Snooping about the time.

On the shores, the nomads are herding the sheep and quickening their pace.

One bird comes alighting at the bow again.

It looks at me before jumping unto the roof. How free it is!

Flapping its shiny wings across the blue sky.

Like my rival, undressing our common love.

Deliberately shames me, humiliates me,

Making me red.

I wish I would die in the light.

Kanbula in late autumn, golden leaves are falling one by one.

塔尔寺磕长头的少女

哥布

据说藏族人一生要到寺庙里磕十万个长头。

——题记

我是来自远方的客人
不太了解青海的礼俗
当我来到塔尔寺
那里有许多人
在长头磕拜
态度虔诚　心无旁骛
其中有一个少女
脸上印着漂亮的高原红
她匍匐又站起
站起又匍匐
反反复复　旁若无人

我是来自远方的客人
不太了解青海的礼俗
当我看见磕长头的少女
我的心为之震撼
你悲苦的时刻
我无缘看见
你饥渴的瞬间
我没有在场
我见证了你一心向佛
我见证了你一心向善
美丽的青海少女
可爱的藏族姑娘
我已然觉察了你内心的无比宁静
我分明感到了你魂中的巨大福祉

BLOWN AWAY AT PROSTRATION OF
A TIBETAN MAIDEN AT TA' ER MONASTERY

Ge Bu

It is said that Tibetans must prostrate themselves in a monastery 100,000 in their lifetime.

—inscription

A tourist from afar.

An ignoramus about Tibetan ways and customs of Tibetan Buddhism.

It struck me

The first time within the Golden—tile Hall of Ta' er Monastery,

To watch a Tibetan lass place her body in a reverentially prone position.

Under the curious eyes of droves of tourists.

An act of extreme submissiveness to the Triple Gems—(Buddha, sutras, monks).

A means of embodying reverence for the Awakened.

Her rosy cheeks, due to heavy dosage of alpine violet rays

Looked to me a sign of innocent blushing

As she prostrated herself time and again,

Hardly aware of the presence of tourists and pilgrims around.

I stood in awe

Of such a moving scene

Of mortals like me so determinedly relinquishing the ego

As she treaded this path.

By casting away desires, lowering her individuality.

Conquering the demons that distracted her.

She was sure to transcend life's sufferings and afflictions.

I stood witness to her devotion to Buddha.

As if I have seen her out of the six realms of incarnation.

To become a Buddha

This lovely Tibetan girl.

I have sensed the incomparable serenity in her.

I have clearly felt the utter bliss overwhelming her.

诗歌

韩丽丽

给你青海湖的蓝色
你的忧郁浸染我的皮肤
给你青藏高原的绿色
你的温暖凝固我的血液
给你牦牛酥油的白色
你的纯净刺盲我的眼睛

在我把所有颜色收回之前
你这悬崖
已经诱我踏出半步
连想象其他颜色的犹豫
都来不及了

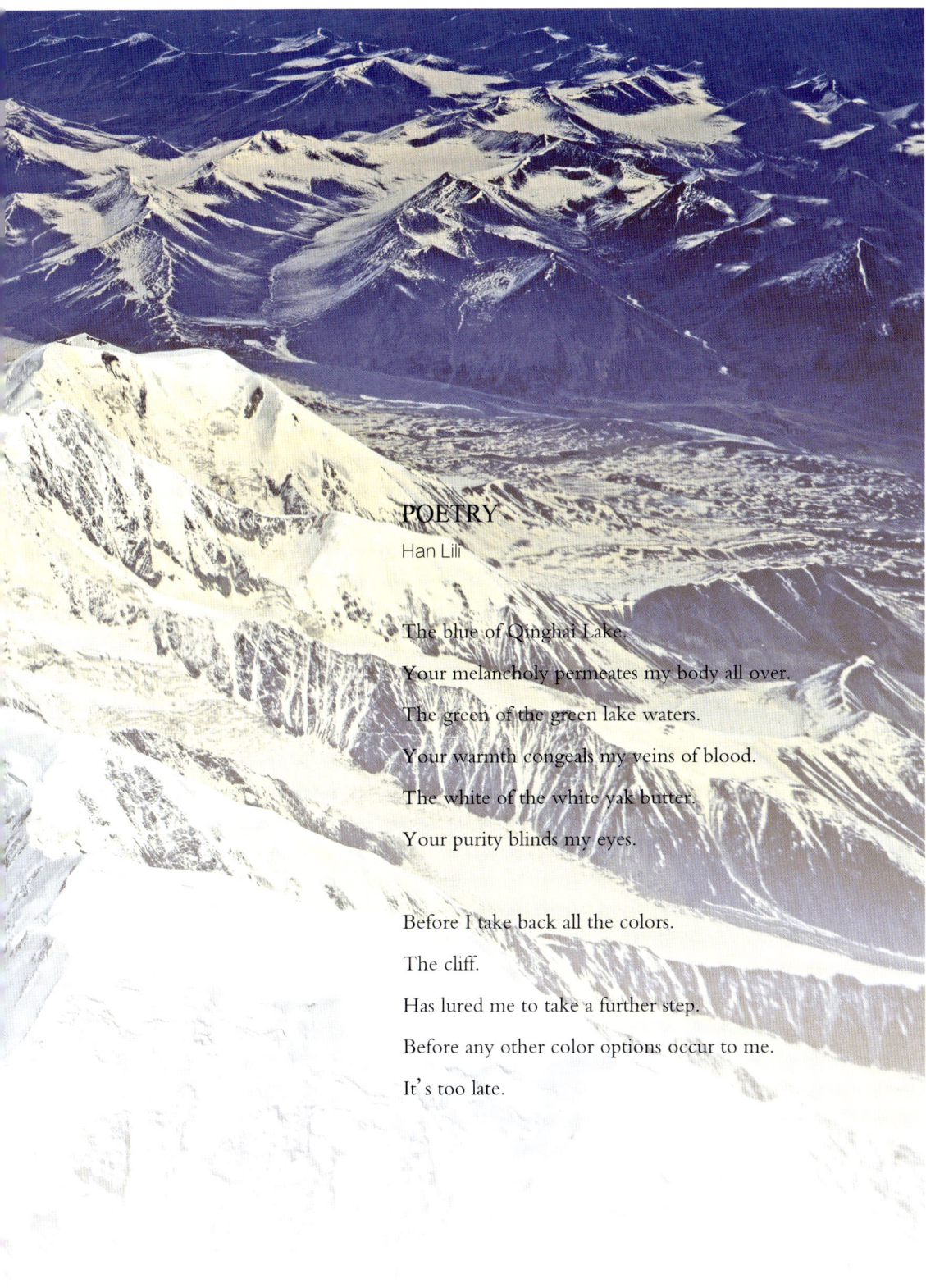

POETRY

Han Lili

The blue of Qinghai Lake.

Your melancholy permeates my body all over.

The green of the green lake waters.

Your warmth congeals my veins of blood.

The white of the white yak butter.

Your purity blinds my eyes.

Before I take back all the colors.

The cliff.

Has lured me to take a further step.

Before any other color options occur to me.

It's too late.

感恩是草原上最朴素的植物
简明

最大的幸福，是赶在黎明前
醒来，把头顶上干净的露水
献给阳光，把身体里千回百转的汁液
也献上！感恩是草原上最朴素的植物
它勤勤恳恳生长，每天长高一寸
一年光景，就能够出落成
处女的模样。草原的旧事物
只生长在新事物上，如同枯草
与热腾腾的牛粪。我相信
阳光每天也是干净的
草原，又何不是如此

GRATITUDE IS THE OFTENEST SEEN PLANTS ON THE GRASSLAND
Jian Ming

No joy appears greater than to awaken before dawn.

And present the dew drops on your head,

To the sunshine, plus the juicy tears.

Thanksgiving is the commonest plant on the grassland.

It grows diligently, an inch taller every day.

It matures but in a year.

Like a baby girl into a full—blown maiden. Old things on the grassland;

Evolve on new things, like withered grass.

Like fresh cow dung. I believe.

The sun is clean every day.

Why not ?

无语青海湖

李轻松

在腹地，在墨绿中，一只清澈的眼睛
或一扇肺叶，都是安静的
我远远地望见她时，似乎不在这个世界

适宜一个人坐下来，从此不再说话
有一种静谧是广大的
我的听力却出奇地好，近在身边的虫鸣
万里之上的翅声
都是如此地入耳，仿佛天籁

这黄的花、青的湖，还有那些奔腾的乌云
随便地说爱她都是轻浮的
我从此凝神了，心无旁骛
一只水鸟站在我的身边
我与你的对视多么保有尊严
现在瓦解的辞藻、颠覆的审美
洗掉了铅华的素颜
今生无须再粉饰。请再给我一点质朴
从此我不敢再任性雕琢……

QINGHAI LAKE—A FANTASTIC INTRODUCTION TO HIGHLAND

Li Qingsong

In the hinterland of Qinghai—a vast expanse of dark blue, like a crystal apple of eye.

Or a lung lobe, all quiet.

Coming into my view the first time, as we drove from a distance, It appeared surreal.

This is a fitting moment to sit down and keep silent.

A serenity of epic proportions reigns.

My hearing is surprisingly good,

Bugs buzz and insects chirp close by.Birds take wings to the skies thousands of miles above.

All distinct, all pleasing to the ear, the sound of nature.

The yellow flowers, the blue water body, and dark clouds surging .

It is frivolous to say that one falls in love with her at first sight.

One must concentrate,

Free from all mundane distractions since.

A water bird is seen next to me.

The mutual gaze at each other proclaims solemnity.

Words disintegrate, notions of aesthetics subverted.

Makeup all removed.

Cosmetics redundant.

No more need to whitewash this life.

I am drawn to a simpler life style.

From today on.

Good both mentally and spiritually.

青海的草原上

李少君

连绵不绝的清风啊
吹拂着连绵不绝的白云
连绵不绝的白云啊
追逐着连绵不绝的羊群
连绵不绝的羊群啊
寻觅着连绵不绝的歌声……

整个草原上，只放牧着一个孤独的
牧羊人

ONE DAY ON THE GRASSLAND IN QINGHAI

Li Shaojun

A breeze.

Continuously chases white clouds.

That stretch out in endless vista.

And flocks of sheep in pursuit.

Restlessly and relentlessly.

As well as songs to be heard in all directions.

The whole grassland herds only one lonely shepherd.

湟源古镇

李小洛

车马和驿站还未出现
我想，我来得有一点唐突
没有想象的大胆和从容
秋天以前，我还是一只青柿子
悬挂在暗处
夜色隆重的树影里

三天之后，我将离开
离开深情的湖水，宽大的草原
一个人走
让你们，多出一些美好的念想
会不会再回来
会不会再一次告别再一次离开
都不重要了。
我只想告诉你
我的爱、我对你的留恋
就停留在此刻
那么悠久，那么漫长……

多么复杂的结构
多么奢华的盛宴
宽大的睡袍和房间
我都不要了
我只携带一顶帐篷
一副听筒、茶色的太阳镜
和一只蜻蜓，或
大雁，共度余生

ONCE–IN–A LIFE EXPERIENCE—ONE DAY IN HUANGYUAN ANCIENT TOWN

Li Xiaoluo

Chariots, horses and post stations have not appeared yet.

I think I arrive not too fittingly.

Without the boldness and calmness of imagination.

Before autumn, I was still a green persimmon.

Hanging where nobody could see.

In the deep shadow of the trees at night.

In three days time, I will leave.

Leave the affectionate lake and the broad grassland.

Alone by myself.

Will this be a perfect excuse

For my returning one day ?

Whether I will make a comeback;

It doesn't matter.

I just want to tell you.

I love you and I will miss you.

I linger and my heart, too.

I truly hate to say adieu.

What a complicated structure!

How sumptuous the feast!

Such a large–sized nightgown and a spacious room.

Mean little to me.

Leave me only one tent.

A pair of handsets and brown sunglasses.

And a dragonfly, or;

A wild geese as company for the rest of my life.

青海

娜夜

大风过后
天　空荡
青海　留出了一片佛的净地

——塔尔寺在风中　酥油花开了
花非花
第一朵叫什么
最后一朵是佛光

这尘世之外的黄昏
——菩提树的可能　舍利子　羊皮书的预言
以及六世达赖仓央嘉措的情歌……

这冥冥中的：因……果……

夕光中
那只突然远去的鹰放弃了谁的忧伤
——人的　还是神的?

QINGHAI

Na Ye

After the gale.

The sky is cleared up.

Qinghai has dedicated a tract of land to Buddha.

The Ta'er Monastery in the wind. Butter flowers blossom.

They are in fact not flowers.

What do you call the first one ?

The last one is Buddha light.

The twilight beyond the earth.

— the possibility of the Bodhi tree, Buddha's relics, prophecy in the Parchment scrolls.

And the love songs of the sixth Dalai Cang Yang Gyatso.

Karma must be at work.

In the twilight.

Whose sadness did the eagle let go ?

Human or divine ?

青海仿民歌

陆正兰

为什么你有时间不看云　　　　　　　你在追问我　我在追问谁
为什么我有蓝天不打雷　　　　　　　追来追去还是那座雪山的美

为什么你仰望天空不追月　　　　　　这世界疑问多如蝴蝶飞
为什么你倾慕水声不流泪　　　　　　这世界给出的答案也太累

你在躲着我　我在躲着谁　　　　　　你在躲着我　我在躲着谁
躲来躲去还是那弯青海湖的水　　　　躲来躲去还是那弯青海湖的水

为什么雄鹰飞了不是罪　　　　　　　这世界疑问多如蝴蝶飞
为什么流沙走了还要回　　　　　　　这世界给出的答案也太累

为什么草原上走路不用伞　　　　　　你在追问我　我在追问谁
为什么你有哥哥我没有妹　　　　　　追来追去还是那座雪山的美

QINGHAI FOLK SONGS

(modeleld on local Hua'er tunes)

Lu Zhenglan

Why do you have leisure, but never stop and
stare at the clouds ?
Why do I command a blue sky, which but
never thunders ?

Why do you look up at the sky instead of
chasing the moon ?
Why do you admire the sound of water but
never cry ?

You're tried to avoid me. Whom am I trying
to avoid ?
Ah, the vast body of water of Qinghai Lake ?

Why is it not a crime for an eagle to fly ?
Why does quicksand come and go ?

Why don't we see herdsmen never use an umbrella on
rainy days ?
Why do you have a brother and I don't have a sister ?

You think me suspicious ? Who else is suspicious, I
wonder.
Ah, the beauty of that snowy mountains.

在坎布拉遇见黄河

栗川

那谪仙诗人沾着微醺的酒气
大笔一挥　顿时
黄河之水自天上奔流而下
千年来蜿蜒于人间
不觉风沙满面　浊浪滔滔

行过岁月的坎坷与康庄
揽一身霜风埃尘
遂成为你流落世间的容颜

坎布拉　丹霞的故乡
在连绵起伏的奇峰上
镂着大地最璀璨的诗行
媲美瑶池祥云　青莲的豪逸

蓦然间　我遇见了你
仿如赤子般的纯净
遂在你的名字中逆溯　逆溯
只见所有的河流不断地奔回
奔回那最初的峰顶

我仿佛听到雪融后的第一滴春泉
循着麋鹿的蹄痕　唤醒
第一茎柔绿　第一朵新花
那开天辟地的一抹微笑
霎时净涤三千世界
人间亦是天上
源头　本来就是明澈无比

I MET WITH THE YELLOW RIVER IN KANBULA

Qin Chuan

The Banished immortal, hammered,

With a stroke of brush, in a flurry,

Enacting the drama of the Yellow River descend to earth,

Flowing east towards the sea for thousands of years.

One could see the muddy torrents surge over his haggard face.

After all these ups and downs;

Our Fallen Fairy moved through the world, though with unearthly ease from attachment,

Belonged profoundly to the earth and its process of change.

Ah, Kanbula.

Your undulating peaks and mind−boggling rock formations.

Sculpted by time,

Comparable almost to the legendary celestial palaces in the Journey to the West.

All of a sudden, you came into sight.

Pure as a newly born infant.

So ethereal in spirit.

I saw all the rivers back and forth.

Before returning to the original summit.

I seem to hear the first drop of spring rain after the snow melts.

Waking up with the elk's hoofing still in my ears.

The first stem branching out, the first flower blossoming

That epoch−making smile;

Cleansing the ten thousand things in an instant.

The earth is heaven as well.

The incomparably clear source.

塔尔寺的天空

三色堇

这里的云朵是从另一座山峰上
飘下来的
那些洁净、安详
一些飘向昨日，一些飘向未来
只有在青海，你才能真切地触摸
它始终未能停住的脚步

洁白是真实的，像极了我当年的嫁衣
在这绝尘的白里
你无法挽住一副温暖的背影
经幡起舞，经筒轻诵
一朵云走过
我在上面写下思念的白天和夜晚
将它们视作美丽的雪山和哈达
视作一幅大雨滂沱的水墨画

这些云朵，莫非是上帝的一种恩赐
它让我站在更高处
感受内心的辽阔，多么喜悦
这就够了
绵远的往事悄悄浮上岸来

UNDER THE SKIES OF TA' ER MONASTERY

San Sejin

Clouds are floating from another mountain.

Auspicious, serene and clean.

Some towards yesterday,

Some into the future.

Only in Qinghai can tangibly touch a piece of it.

Although they are in constant motion. unfolding

spontaneously.

Pure white is real, much like my wedding dress

commissioned for the big occasion.

In this unearthly white.

You can't hold a warm back.

The prayer flags dance and the scriptures sing softly.

One speck of cloud passes by.

On which I write down my whims, my remembrances of

day and night.

Which I think of as beautiful snow-capped mountains and

Hada scarves.

Or as a large canvass of traditional landscape painting.

Are these clouds a gift from God ?

I simply feel I am standing taller.

My mind enlightened, my heart blessed.

That's enough.

Events, experiences and associations crowd into this moment.

雪域

——致青藏高原

沈奇

这　不是借住的风景
这是世界的原在

高上去——
四千米、五千米的海拔
留存于生命初稿中的雪意
才不会　轻易融化

高上去——
高过欲望　高过
虚构的荣誉
让物质的肉身
复归　软弱的实际

然后　在
细草般的呼吸里
开始心虚　开始畏惧
开始举念：要证明点什么
相信些……什么

然后　再
回到低处
我们毕竟是低处的动物
——那些欲望
那些荣誉
那些诱惑难挡的堕落
谁的生命　能
完全忽略？

可那些接近过天路的
人们啊　又有谁能忘却
——那蓝天绝望的蓝
那白云无私的白
那只与风对话的经幡
那丈量信仰极限的香客们
磕长头的身影　以及
牦牛　眼中的深寒？！

高上去　再
低下来——
没有谁能真正改变
这人世的戏码

只是　在此后的生命中
你灵魂的深处　便多了一道
不能退却的雪线
并　重新向往
那朵　仅仅活在想象中的
圣洁的雪莲花……

FALLING FOR SOME OF THE MOST SUBLIME SCENERY IN A SNOWLAND

Shen Qi

To the Qinghai—Tibet Plateau.

Make no mistake this is a borrowed view.

This plateau forms part of a single cosmic watershed.

Up high—

Four kilometers, five kilometers above sea level.

Snow encoded in my poems,

Won't melt easily.

Up high—

Higher than desire.

The every day facts of man—made rank and honor;

Are belied.

Irredeemably.

And then.

In the weakness of grass—like breath.

We are made to feel uneasy, even a little

inapprehensible.

The bad need to argue for the ego that fades;

To prove a point barely untenable.

And then.

Fly away, back to the low land.

After all, we are low—lying beings, suitable for more

settled life.

The necessary baggage of cravings,

Consciences of distinction and decorum.

The irredeemable depravity of irresistible temptation.

Whose current life can be lived,

Nebulous and beyond ?

But those who have journeyed on the Heavenly

Road.

Can never forget;

The blue highland sky that makes one despair of.

The white clouds moving errantly.

The prayer banners whispering sutras in the wind.

The pilgrims who measure the extent of their

devoutness.

By prostrating themselves in a headlong prone

position before the statues of Buddha untiringly,

And everybody can tell the forthcoming bitter wind

in the eyes of yaks ? !

Ascend and descend.

Slip back in to our ways—

No one can really rewrite and reenact.

The drama of the world.

Only for the rest of my life.

There's one snowline in the depths of my soul.

One that will never retreat.

And look forward to watching again.

The holy snow lotus flower

The wonder evoked In my imagination, albeit.

丹噶尔

汪剑钊

丹噶尔，一只反扣高原的白海螺，
撞击，摩擦，产生微妙的斑点。

唐蕃争战遗留的战靴，
缓缓升起一朵偈子似的莲花。

蹭去折戟的尘垢，湟鱼
在螺壳深处衔紧海水的记忆。

仓央嘉措为皎洁的月亮押上藏地的韵脚，
情歌在每一块青石板中沁出。

而鹦鹉的皮影在黑边牌坊下雕刻时光，
排灯照彻皮绣的每一根纤维。

丹噶尔在历史的老街上随风飘成传说，
驼铃比郁金香更灿烂地开放于旷野……

SEEING DANGER UP CLOSE

Wang Jianzhao

Dangar, an inverted white conch that buckles the plateau.
Impact, friction, produce subtle spots.

Cavalry boots, redolent of the hostilities between Tang and Tibet in
medieval times.
A lotus flower arising like a clover.

Rubbing off the dirt of the halberd, naked carp
Retain the memory in the depths of the oceans.

The sixth Dalai, Cangyang Gyatso rhymed his love songs,
Out of each bluestone paving the streets.

And parrots in the shadow puppets, carved by the passage of time.
The lanterns illuminate every fiber in the leather embroidery display.

Dangar, the ancient town, passes into history as a legend.
Camel caravans ring out sonorously in the wilderness, blossoming
more luxuriantly than tulips.

噫吁嚱！一个行者

——致昌耀

宋琳

你听着太阳蜂窝的声息
入夜时河与湟汇合的声息
你手持圭状木棍，像一个竖亥或大章
行走在盐与硫黄的地区
流沙中露出古陶罐的双耳
吹着骷髅的空穴来风

海市蜃楼为你开启天街的拱门
魔鬼城的红舌头把恐惧许配给你
土碉堡里的隐形人邀你同饮
最小的湖仙要用双乳做你的暖炉
带你飞渡弱水，扶摇直上

虚空复虚空，尘埃和野马的远乡
有金冠辉耀于万仞山的巅顶
而下面，蝼蚁疾走于青冢之丘
某个死，美丽如一位判官
等你在歧路口，且备好了
来世的饷宴与笙歌

你走着，不为所动。当你迷路
大荒西经中的珍禽异兽就出来
做你贞吉的向导。销魂地，当你瞥见
一首诗——那稀薄空气里的暗香
渴意就化作一片梅子林

你贫穷，你消瘦如一杆竹
走着向上与向下的同一条命途
噫吁嚱！一个行者
噫吁嚱！鸿蒙的过客
今夕何夕？卡日曲的鸣泉朝你逶迤而来
你在月下洗着，赤条条地洗着
复陶醉于雪水中骨骼的铮铮

LOOK,HERE COMES A BIKKU!

Song Lin

Tuning in to the sizzling of the sun's beehive,

And the gurgling confluence of the two rivers;

A walking stick in hand, like some legendary figure,

You plod your way amidst the territories of salt marsh and sulphur.

From the flowing sand surface two handles of an antiquated amphora;

Through the orifices of some skulls blows an eerie wind.

The mirage reveals for you the arches leading to the celestial roads;

The devil's city sticks out its red tongue to impress a fear upon you;

The earthen fortress is home to some stealthy wights toasting to you;

The tiniest river spirit warms your body with her dangling breasts,

Like a bridge over troubled waters, making you soar on high.

All is vain; all is empty. The distant homeland of dust and vapour

Is crowned in gold upon its blade—like summits,

While down below, trivial creatures skid along the green undulating grave mounds.

Some figure of death, gaudy as a judge in the netherworld,

Awaits you at the crossroads, preparing you for

An afterworld of feasts and singing.

So you walk on, not moved a whit. When lost

In the barrens, mythical fouls and beasts present themselves

As auspicious guides. Entranced, you see

Poetry before you—faint fragrance seeping through the rarified air—

And all your thirst becomes transmuted into a satisfying plum forest.

In willed poverty, emaciated as a bamboo stalk,

You plod a path reaching simultaneously up and down.

So, the Dharma man you are!

So, a passerby in this world!

And what a night it is, that the brook of Kariqu meanders singing towards you ?

Bathing in the moonlight, your naked frame in Zen—like simplicity,

You imbibe the pure ecstasy melting from the snow.

青海

唐欣

火焰山　火焰已凝固
倒淌河　河水向西流
途经一座干净的小镇
想象我在这里度过一生

青稞酒　我喝不醉
但我的舌头发硬
喉咙哽塞　这是否
也是李白他们常干的事

鹰在头顶飘着
草原伸开　乌云翻卷
摸出烟　我忘了带火
一抬头　我看见了雪山

玉树　果洛　好听的名字
留待下次吧　我肯定
还要来　还有鸟岛
以后我也去那儿飞

QINGHAI

Tang Xin

On the Flame Mountain, fire has subsided.

Daotang River(Westward Flowing), passing by a namesake compact town,

Beckons me to settle down.

For the remainder of my life.

I can't end up thoroughly drunk with highland barley wine.

But my tongue is stiff.

And my throat has gone hoarse.

Is it the same case with Fallen Fairy of the Tang？

An eagle is sailing overhead.

The grassland stretches out without end. The sky is overcast.

Reaching out to find the cigarette, I forget to bring along lighter with me.

Looking up, I see the snow-capped mountain.

Yushu, Guoluo-what a ring to these names in Amdo!

Good excuse for another visit, I'm sure.

And Bird Island-the stop-over for birds in migration

I will return to fly with wild geese and white swans in the future.

杂事诗·在大银塔前

徐江

传说宗喀巴诞生,从脐带滴血处长出一株白旃檀树,其十万片叶子上每片自然现出一尊狮子吼佛像。

宗二十二岁,其母给远在西藏的他,寄去白发一绺,说"吾今年迈体衰,盼儿务必返里一晤"。宗为学佛决意不返,给慈母和姊姊各寄去用自己鼻血绘成的自画像一幅、狮吼佛像一轴,嘱其母:"若在我出生之地以十万尊狮子吼佛像及菩提树(即白旃檀树)为胎藏建一佛塔,则如同亲晤儿面。"宗母在信徒资助下,按儿子在信中的意思,建成了佛塔,以寄托思念之情。这就是"大银塔"。后来人们又依塔建寺,这就有了"塔尔寺"。

MISCELLANEOUS POEMS IN FRONT OF THE BIG SILVER PAGODA

Xu Jiang

Tsongkhapa, the founder of the Gelug school of Tibetan Buddhism, was born in 1357. According to one tradition, a sandalwood tree grew up where drops of blood from Tsongkhapa's umbilical cord had fallen (where the monastery is now) this tree became known as the "Tree of Great Merit." The leaves and the bark of this tree were reputed to bear impressions of the Buddha's face and various mystic syllables and its blossoms were said to give off a peculiarly pleasing scent.

At the age of 22, his mother sent him a lock of white hair in a letter as far away as Tibet, saying, "My health declines rapidly this year. I urge you to return to see the last of me." Tsongkhapa, engrossed in rigorous monastic practice, lingered against her wish, sending his mother and sister a self-portrait painted with their own nosebleeds and a shaft of the lion roaring Buddha, instructing her mother "If you have a temple with a stupa built, as well a bohdi tree planted (white sandalwood trees) in the place where I was born, fancy you are sitting face to face with your own son." With the aid of local believers, her mother did accordingly to satisfy her yearning for family reunion, hence the origin of the Ta'er Monastery.

大银塔里包住的白旃檀树，据说到现在仍然活着。

宗母直到去世，也没能再见到儿子一眼。

导游讲完上面内容时，我有一点哽咽。

还好，马非已随着香客们到门口转经去了，老彭也到走廊上拍照。再度注目了银塔，走到殿外，我点上支烟，悄悄地等眼中的潮湿褪去。

想起早年读圣经，读耶稣下十字架一段，以及读《日瓦戈医生》中《客西马尼的林园》一诗，甚至二十多岁那年写我自己的《客西马尼随想》组诗的时候……这些年，许多事情是一直不变的。连酸楚也是一样——不为"偶像"，是为"偶像"曾生而为人。

那么，不变真好。

The white sandalwood tree in the big silver tower is said to be still alive.

His mother never saw her son again until she died.

When the guide finished, I felt a little choked up.

Fortunately, my friend Ma Fei was absent being lead away with other tourists and another friend, Lao Peng was busy taking photos somewhere. Casting a reverential glance at the tower, I stepped outside the hall, lit a cigarette and quietly waited for the dampness in my eyes to fade.

I recalled reading Doctor Zhivago and the Bible a couple of years ago, chancing upon a passage of Jesus crucified upon the cross, I even wrote a poem entitled "The Garden of Gethsemane" in my twenties. Over the years, I have still stuck to my reverence for two saints—Tsongkhapa and Jesus, both of humble origin, ultimately attaining to sainthood whose works and teachings become central for Christianity and Tibetan Buddhism, two great live religions of our modern world. One difference: Tsongkhaba wrote extensively on Buddhism and his interpretation and exegesis has become a major focus of Gelug scholasticism.

岁末，想起德州草原

宋长玥

风中的房子
旧雪和漫过缓坡的长草。我分开两个世界：
白天和黑夜。
它们是安静的——青海湖北侧
牧人赶着自己的影子走向大湖腹地。
以远，天鹅举步
沙洲冷。

太阳在左。
谁是它心爱的人。金露梅收起黄金，
银露梅送走银子。
牛角下一片青草荒芜辽远，这是绝大多数的命运
他选择的生活
面目全非，是他的，又不是他的。
这些卑微的尘埃
被神考验过，自己背负着自己的重——
他们纯洁了。

而隐身牧道的背影归于沉静，
德州多么美。

DEZHOU GRASSLAND: YEAR-END REMINISCENCES

Song Changyue

The wind-blown huts sit on
The aging snow covering a slope brimming with grass. I divide up two worlds:
Night and day.
They each are serene—in the north of the Qinghai Lake,
A shepherd is driving his own shadow towards the heart of the lake.
Further off, the swans are trudging
On a cold, bleak sandbar.

The sun is seated to my left—
But whom is it in love with? The golden cinquefoils have withdrawn their shine,
And the silvery ones parted with their sheen.
The cattle horns overlook a vast field of sparse growth, the fate of most folks,
Their self-chosen lot to graze on.
Utterly defaced, it is his, yet not his.
Tested by the gods, and walking on the way of the cross,
They are being slowly purged of impurities.

The shepherds' path sinks back into its obscure meditation,
Leaving the Dezhou Grassland alone to its beauty.

在大通峡谷
叶玉琳

不要以为这个季节
它是完美中的最完美，万山中的唯一
也不要以为这个世界
鲜花开过就绚烂，尘埃飘过就岑寂
在这幽深的丛林，我只循着一个方向
阳光遮挡着它
道路是那么曲折，漫无边际

远方有大鹰唤我
声音哽咽，像多年前的朋友
每一株圆柏都在问我
你究竟在寻找什么
雨水酿成了林中之蜜
星宿投进了新的湖泊
而我，究竟是为了什么来到这里
被遥远的天灯凝望了一夜
被孤独的空谷拥抱了一夜
我像一匹喷血的鬃马，旋转，飞奔
一点一点地接近高原蓝天
并在那里交出了半个梦

风继续吹。冰雪就要覆盖土地
带走察汗河两岸
成熟的庄稼和牛羊的热流
人世间的悲与喜
就像刚卸下外衣的浆果和灌木
不要以为它跌进了一个盐湖
就不要重回山林
我的马儿最终要跃出水面
它的翅膀将盖住曲曲弯弯的归途

DATONG CANYON

Ye Yulin

Fancy not this is the only season to track down the canyon.

Although it is at its spectral best, no doubt, the canyon of canyons.

And fancy not the wild nameless flowers.

After a spell of luxuriant blossoming,

And return to dust, silent forever.

In this lush canyon where a profusion of fauna and flora obscuring the sunshine,

Drawing in legions of explorers and hikers like me

I follow the trails threading the meandering Datong River.

These trails, tortuous and tough, are not to be dodged by all means.

An eagle is calling me in the distance.

In a choking voice, like a friend parted years ago.

Cypresses that I pass by are inquisitive.

What exactly are you looking for ?

They wonder.

Rain water is the honey in the forest.

Meteors fall into the new lake.

And why on earth do I trip here ?

Gazing at the celestial vaults all night.

Embraced by the lonely empty valley all night.

I gallop like a bloodshot horse with a mane.

A little closer to the blue sky on the plateau.

And handing in half a dream there.

The wind continues to blow. Snow and ice will soon blanket the land.

Whisking away all the crops, the heat waves, cattle and sheep,

On the banks of Chahan River.

The joys and sorrows of the world.

Like berries and shrubs that have just taken off their coat.

Fancy not since you stumble into a lake.

You would never return to the mountains.

My horse will eventually jump out of the water.

To cover and hide the winding trials home with its wings.

青海湖

叶舟

心灵的继承者！这野花沸腾的水面多么宁静。

这野花沸腾的水面一如往昔。
深蓝色的钢板，挂着人类之巢
一炉深入的孤独
像热烈飞行的煤炭。
青海湖，上升的女神——
大地粗糙的养育是多么神圣。
扑天而起的鸦群
我纪念最后的信使一再推迟。

心灵的继承者，天空的经册苍白无字。
寒凉的码头
使日光沉入的鱼群，醉生梦死。
哦，如果八月是一道谶言——
我要洗净我的罪恶
我要赞颂，人的劳作。

QINGHAI LAKE

Ye Zhou

Heir of the soul! A riot of wild ripples,
As always!

Waters seethe in the lake in a riot of wild ripples
in full blossom.
A colossal steel plate, dark blue, on which hangs
the cradle of humanity.
The gigantic furnace of loneliness
Is like a burning coal nugget fervent in flight!
Qinghai Lake, a Goddess in the rise—
Rising from the soil like a colossal doughnut,
How sacred, how impulsively the earth has raised
her offspring!
Crows flap their wings to cover the whole sky,
mourning
My last messengers long after this homage was
due.

Inheritors of the soul, the celestial sutras are
without a single character.
A cold dockside
Looks on the sunlit shoals of fish in a drunken a
spree.
Oh, if August were a prophecy—
Then I would cleanse my sins.
I will sing in praise of man's labours.

野蜂凄艳
蝴蝶呼喊
一阵阵高入天堂的狂雪引人入胜。
所以青海，以及你美丽的正午
像十万散失的马群——
披挂了精神的经幡。
哦，我内心的气象和海拔
将毁于一旦。

青海湖，你野花沸腾的水面多么宁静。

曙光初现的女人传递了繁殖之事。
神祇的筵席，必是
鹰击之下一场功课的结局——
如果没有人咳血朗诵
我将如何收拾起爱戴的泪水？
所以青海，一次遥远的眺望
多么痉挛。

心灵的继承者！请继续了悲痛
继续了坚持的体温。

世纪垂照，在每一个黄昏，请让我想起青海之青
这野花沸腾的水面多么宁静。

Wild bees are sunk in sorrow.

Butterflies are wailing in a distraught mood.

Waves of snow from heaven are absolutely
fascinating.

Qinghai, beauteous at noontide,

Like myriad stray horses—

Decked fully with prayer flags.

Oh, my inner clime and soul's elevation.

Will be lost forever.

Qinghai Lake, what tranquility of your waters,
blooming in a riot of wild ripples!

At dawn a woman gives birth to a baby, the
perennial tale of human evolution.

The feasting time of the gods

Ends with the fierce eagle's raid—

If the poet fails to cough up blood in reading his
poems,

How can I wipe away my tears of love ?

Qinghai, what a spasm

Is my every gaze at your face!

Heir of the soul! Keep on grieving—

Keep your long-standing body temperature.

At the start of each century, at every dusk, please
remind me of Qinghai's verdure,

And the tranquility of the waters blooming in a
riod of wild ripples!

泼墨狂草，坎布拉

张默

坎布拉，你是面七彩晶莹的镜子
冠以独特的丹霞地貌，在青海昂首耸立着
咱们驱车在环山蜿蜒多变的公路上
向下看是一个个澄清无比的湖泊
四处参差层叠连绵挺拔的怪石
让人目不暇接，而不停地张望
生怕那川流不息大笔狂草的绝景
悠悠然，一骨碌从眼底飞逸

每每在山路上快速地向上攀升
我的视线恍惚绕着李家峡电厂跳探戈
从最初触及灰色巨大的建筑基座，逐渐缩小
再缩小
木立四周的柱状群峰，更是雄浑幽僻
那一折折剪不断十分苍翠的山色
正面被阳光倾泻得更灿亮，但方向的侧影
似在埋怨自己经年无人闻问的私密
坎布拉，你是我的诗早早下注的秋声赋

AN EXCURSION TO KANBULA

Zhang Mo

Kanbula, you look to me like a huge mirror.

Reflecting flaming—red mountains

That meet the turquoise waters of Lijiaxia Reservoir

With your unique Danxia rock formations,

You stand tall in an outlying desert

The beautiful greens, purples, sapphires and blues of the mountains,

Waters and sky over Kanbula, it stands with its head held high in Qinghai.

We drove on the nervous—sweat—inducing road,

Snaking up through the park's peaks

Where we looked down to gorge on a slew of limpid lakes.

Weird rock configurations at every turn.

We climbed the long wooden staircases up to the vast statue of Buddha

At the end of the stairs.

The views from here were simply a knock—out.

As we bumped on the treacherous road.

My eyes danced the tango at Lijiaxia Power Plant in a trance.

From the massive base at first, it gradually shrank out of sight.

The column of peaks loomed majestic and mind—boggling.

The sunny side of the mountains,

Basking in the sunshine, but the opposite side, looking gloomier.

As if complaining about its long—held claustration

Kanbula, you are the best tribute to autumn in Qinghai.

听花儿

阿毛

为了在天上，我住过扎在天边的帐房
你唱的花儿，惊醒了我身体里的电闪雷鸣
你唱的花儿，重现了我灵魂里的天蓝地绿
为了在地上，我躺过镶在地上的河床
你唱的花儿，在清点我的穷光阴
你唱的花儿，在翻理我的细柔肠
为了在诗里，我翻过刻在青铜上的黄卷
泪水涟涟啊，
又美又绝望！

LISTENING TO LOCALS SING HUA'ER(Folk Songs)

A Mao

In order to ascend to the sky, I have lodged in a hut on the horizon.

Your melodies have awakened the thunder and lightning in me.

Recreating the blue sky and the green earth in my soul.

In order to be close to nature, I lay on the riverbed inlaid on the ground.

Your singing has settled the accounts of my poverty.

Touching where my heart is tenderest.

In order to write the most beautiful piece of poem,

I have thumbed through the yellow scrolls engraved on bronze.

Tears stream down my cheeks.

Beautiful and desperate!

青海湖诗歌广场

查干

湖水还是辽阔的湛蓝

如同歌诗

眺望的眸子

她长长的睫毛一旦闪动

野花和云絮就开始抒写

人类情诗

地球牧歌

这艺术的　磅礴的　铜雕群

是谁哲思的创意呢

在皓首雪山眷顾的

青青草地上

它们安静地耸立

并且凝视　凝视一种

诗之大美

从此这里是诗之故乡

使日月安静

QINGHAI LAKE POETRY SQUARE

Cha Gan

The vast expense of the lake.

Majestic and soul−stirring like a song and a poem.

Once her long eyelashes flicker.

Wild flowers and clouds begin to write.

Love poems.

Pastoral songs of the earth.

The high artistic point,

Is the bronze sculptures of 24 world poets.

That have attained to world renown.

Whose brain child is this square dedicated to poetry ?

Overlooked by snow−capped mountains in the distance.

On the green grass.

They stand tall and quiet.

The poetic stare, sort of.

The ultimate beauty of poetry.

Ever since, this is the Mecca of poetry.

That charms both the sun and the moon.

高原之夜

古筝

在高原，缓慢爱上我
富足的阳光爱上我修长缓慢的身影。
一切有序地缓慢向前。

在高原，青草没有边界，羊群像白云一样缓缓漂移。
星空开成一朵朵美丽的格桑花。我看见
那个距我最近的人，他眼里的火种
将夜晚点燃。

高原之夜，多像一个波澜宽阔的男人
敞开巨大的胸襟，将尘世的一切，以及我小小的愿望
全部揽入怀中。

夜好深啊，群山环抱中的西宁市，像我一样
抱住一个甜蜜的八月。

在强行爱我的高原面前，我缓慢地低下头
在坚决把我带入慢节奏的高原，我扬起一张雨水的脸。

ONE NIGHT SPENT ON THE QINGHAI–TIBET PLATEAU

Gu Zheng

On the plateau, gentle pace of living falls in love with me.

The bumper sunshine favors my slender and slow–moving figure.

Everything crawls in an orderly way;

On the plateau, the grass grows luxuriantly to the end of the world.

Sheep graze lazily and leisurely like white clouds.

The starry sky blossoms into beautiful Sims Azalea.

I see the man closest to me, the spark in his eyes.

Sets the night ablaze.

The night on the plateau resembles a giant.

Who embraces all creatures as well as my little wishes.

In his huge arms.

Night deepens as Xining is surrounded by mountains, just like me.

Holds fast to a sweet August.

I bow my head before an impetuous and bossy plateau.

And raise my face, fully wet with rain water to come to terms with

the force locking me into the slow–paced plateau.

青海湖，你是我的爱人

哈森

青海湖，你是我的爱人。远远地，
你那绿松石般的宁静与明亮
吸引了我。我怀着无尽遐想
不远千里，来到你的面前。

青海湖，你哪里是水，分明是
天地间伫立的碧蓝色屏障。
疲惫的我，真想依偎你身旁
除去一路的风尘与劳倦。

青海湖，神授的土地，无疑是
神灵在指引着我的心，膜拜你
五彩的经幡，沉默的嘛呢石
还有仓央嘉措的传说。

青海湖，脚步到达之前，歌声
早已抵达。如果一个地方
与信仰和爱有关，即便有
万重障碍，也不能将我阻挠。

青海湖，你是我的爱人。包容
我的任性、我的感伤、我的泪水
我的无助、我的疼痛、我的怯懦……
你的浩瀚中，我变成一只自由的水鸟。

青海湖，自从与你相遇，所有的水
已然不再是水，更谈不上是湖泊。
在你的目光里我找到了上世的牵引
在你的庇护下我认定了今生的宿命。

QINGHAI LAKE, MY LOVE

Ha Sen

Qinghai Lake, my love—how your
Turquoise cool and brilliance
Drew me! And how, on endless fancy's flight,
I've traversed the distances all the way to you.

You are not just a body of water—no, but
An azure screen erected under the sun.
In my fatigue I long to lean on you,
To wash away my traveler's grime.

Qinghai Lake, a true godsend you are.
Driven at heart by the deities, I pay my homage
The iridescent prayer flags tethered to your sides,
The Mani stones speaking goodwill in silence,
And Tsangyang Gyatso, the poet-Lama in love.

Qinghai Lake, my songs have reached you
Before my steps did. Nothing can steer me astray
On my pilgrimage to love and faith,
Be there ten thousand obstacles.

Qinghai Lake, my love, do forgive
My whims, my blues, my tears.
Befriend me, soothe me, and hearten me:
Set me in flight in your wild water kingdom.

Qinghai Lake, ever since our rendezvous,
No other waters are waters anymore, let alone lakes.
In your soulful gaze I come to know my karma;
In your sweet asylum, I come to grasp my destiny.

黄河石

刘慧儒

黄河石嵌在黄河的窟窿
黄河石知道黄河所有的孔窍
黄河石成就了黄的玲珑
庄子可曾说过
黄河石是黄河低沉的嗓音

黄河石与黄河摩挲抚慰
黄河石与黄河传递彼此的搏动
黄河石与黄河是一种难舍的契合
万千年的切磋
寻找着最佳弧度和弧度的圆润
黄河的体温中有矿苗的质感
黄河石的肤下有河流的肌理
水的记忆留在了石头纹路
倒影里，星象酝酿着最后的定位
传说中的河图
是黄河石和黄河私情的信物

你所知道的黄河
那是没有窟窿的黄河
你见过的黄河石
都不是黄河石
因为黄河石不会离开黄河
因为
没有黄河石的黄河
就不是黄河了

YELLOW RIVER ROCKS

Liu Huiru

Grotesque rocks stud the Yellow River's orifices;
They know all of the river's nooks and crannies;
They complete its thousand charms.
Chuang Tzu might well have said
That the rocks are the Yellow River's bass voice line.

The river and the rocks fondle one another:
They exchange their vibrant pulses.
Soulmates to one another, they have
Worked at the best curvatures and the best smoothness
For eons.
The river's body temperature is borne by its bonanzas;
Its wrinkles are lined over the rocks' surfaces;
The rocks are lined with the memories of the currents.
The reflections of the stars are in the final pangs of alignment:
The Oracle of the *I Ching*
Is the river's love token to its rocks.

The Yellow River that you know of
Is not the hollow creek which I know.
The Yellow River rocks which you have seen
Are not the real ones either.
Real Yellow River rocks never leave their Mother,
Nor is their Mother
Herself anymore
When bereft of her offspring.

转经筒前的诗歌朗诵会

鲁若迪基

母亲手里的转经筒
放大千万倍
就成这个样子了
今夜，我们就在这巨大的转经筒前
为世界祈福
让诗歌的声音
在清凌凌的黄河畔
轻轻响起
此刻，战争的硝烟散去
饥饿的人们都有了面包和水
月光铺满回家的路
孩子在母亲怀里
含着奶头睡去了
一切都静下来
树屏住呼吸
遥远的星星
也听到了我们的心跳
那些沉默的
开始比土地沉默
那些辽阔的
开始比天空辽阔

POETRY READING BY THE PRAYER WHEELS

Luruo Diji

Look—they are the same as the little prayer wheel

Spun in a my mother's hand,

Except a thousand times bigger.

Tonight, let us pray by these mammoths of wheels

For world peace and prosperity.

May the voices of poetry resound

By this rare crystalline stretch

Of the Yellow River.

Now, with the battle smoke dispersed,

And the hungry blessed with bread and water;

With the moonlight scattered on our way home,

And the children fast asleep,

Sucking at their mothers' breasts,

Peace reigns all over.

The trees are holding their breaths,

And our heartbeats have become audible

Even to the stars light—years away,

So the quiet gets quieter

Than the soil—bed,

And the vast expanses become

Broader than the sky—dome.

寻找卓玛

曲近

沿着王洛宾的歌声一路向上
寻找卓玛
寻找打劫了歌王之心的人
寻找一朵格桑花

青海湖边
金银滩前
飘逸而来的人儿
她手捧哈达
她高举酒碗
她一曲情歌让我忘记回家

醉看羞赧的花
每一朵都叫格桑
醉看牧羊姑娘
每一个都是卓玛

我问这是不是传说
青海湖笑而不答

WHERE IS ZHUOMA,THE TIBETAN MAID THAT CHARMED OUR FOLK SONGS KING?

Qu Jin

To the sound of Wang Luobin, the reputed King of Folk Songs in Western China,

I set my mind to look for Zhuoma, the famed Tibetan girl

That won his heart.

Inspiring him to compose the popular song "In the Far distant Place"

A theme that has immortalized this land called Qinghai

The Sims Azalea of the our beauty-obsessed world .

Qinghai Lake.

The eternal venue in honor of the girl-Gold and Silver Grassland.

The mandatory Qinghai experience.

A sumptuous ritual is enacted each day dawns

For our benefit—us tourists.

Zhuoma, or her incarnation, holds Hada in one hand.

The wine jar and bowl in another.

Sings out the usual love theme that maximizes the pastoral magic.

Drunk and dizzy, each wild flower to me is a Sims Azalea,

Each girl, a Zhuoma.

I asked if it was a legend.

Qinghai Lake smiled but did not answer.

土族村，或二十分钟的新郎

凸凹

梦吗？在一群美丽的土族阿姑簇拥下，我再一次
做了一回新郎。青海，互助县，一次偶然相遇
也有彩虹的绚丽？那些，在庭院中间
跳安昭舞、玩轮子秋、赛马、唱花儿的小伙姑娘
多像他们自己：那舞蹈的身子，那音乐的脸
那时，瞬间的一个臆想，居然成为接下来的
现实：我万万没想到，那天，二十多个同伴中
我和另一位幸运者，竟成了民俗村上午十时的
新郎。隔得那么近，我怎能在一帘红纱下，选出那
陌生而纯丽的异族女？穿着新郎官衣裳
接住抛来的香袋，妇唱夫和，妻舞夫蹈
甚至，还闹了洞房。捏着我送的红包
伴郎伴娘一个劲夸我是最好的郎。噢那天
只要背过新娘，只要洞房里的床不说话
所有的人看见我，就像看见真正的新郎——甚至
午饭时，我的新娘还能远远寻来，凭着那只香袋的
气味找到我，为我把一碗又一碗青稞酒唱响
"那二十分钟表演，为什么竟奢侈到
用一首诗来表达怀念？"写完这首诗才发觉
我必须虚拟一个老婆提问，并设法找到生活的答案

AT A MONGOL VILLAGE
WHERE I WAS A TWENTY-MINUTE BRIDEGROOM

Tu Ao

Was this a dream ? —That, rallied around by Mongour girls of astonishing beauty, I was a bridegroom for a second time in my life. Beautiful Huzhu County, Qinghai!—where a chance encounter would strike up a rainbow-like romance!

How much themselves they were—highland lads and lasses dancing, frolicking, riding and singing out in the open:

Their gyrating bodies and musical faces imparted to me a fantasy soon brought to pass:

Never had I dared to think that I, with another lucky boy, would soon be picked from the twenty-some tourists as mock-grooms at the Folk Culture Village at ten o'clock that morning!

So close, yet so strange, were the pristine, exotic bride candidates lined up before me—from where whom should I pick ?

There I stood, in my groom's garments, caught off-guard by the sachet tossed to me, singing along with her, pounding clumsily to her dance moves, while one great thing led to another, and we eventually cemented our wedlock in her bridal chamber.

Both the groomsmen and bridesmaids called me the best groom ever—with my red packets in hand, of course.

Oh, what a day!—when, as long as I had carried her on my back, and the bride's bed would not betray me, I must have passed as a real bridegroom in everybody's eye!

And better yet—when it came to lunchtime, my bride would follow the scent of the sachet and find her way to me, singing toasts over cups after cups of highland barley wine.

"How does a twenty-minute performance deserve the remembrance of a poem ?" I asked myself.

Only when I had finished writing, did I realize: I must think up a wife to direct this question to, then dig at the truth about life.

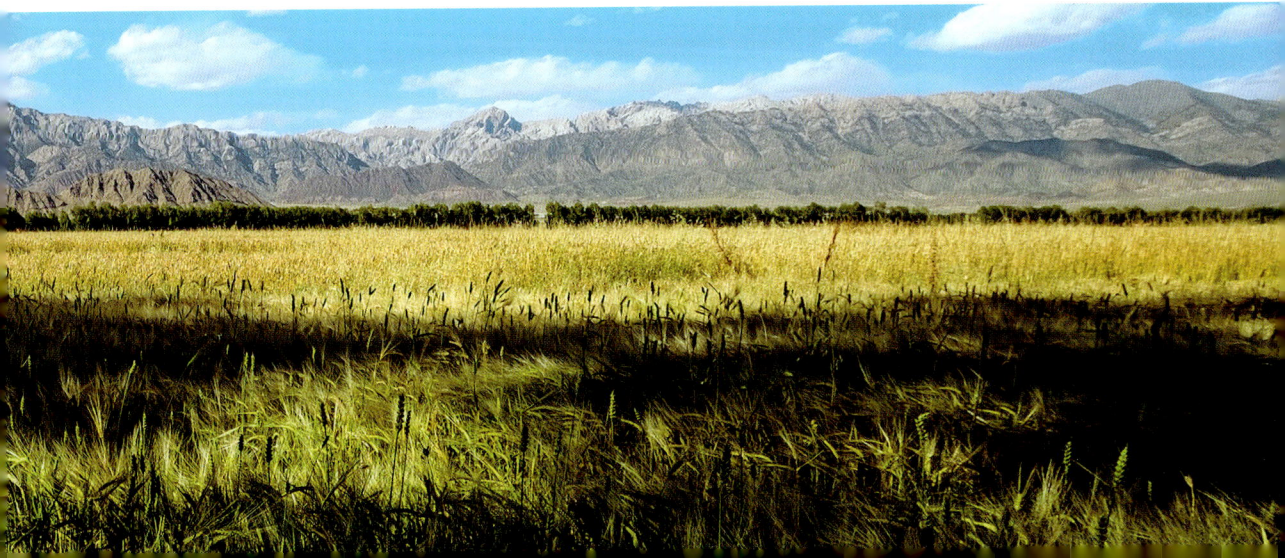

格桑花

王琦

阳光下，一支格桑花在摇曳
夏天将过去，很快花瓣儿就会回到泥土
这瞬间的过程，只有相爱的人才能发现
短暂的一生，红颜即将褪尽
我们才在一朵即将凋零的花前找到替身

我们是彼此的花瓣儿，最精华的部分
都开给了对方。很快，我们也要回归大地
在高原深处安息。
唉，秋风说起就起了，心中的格桑花
一瓣一瓣儿落下，让我想起你脸上的皱纹

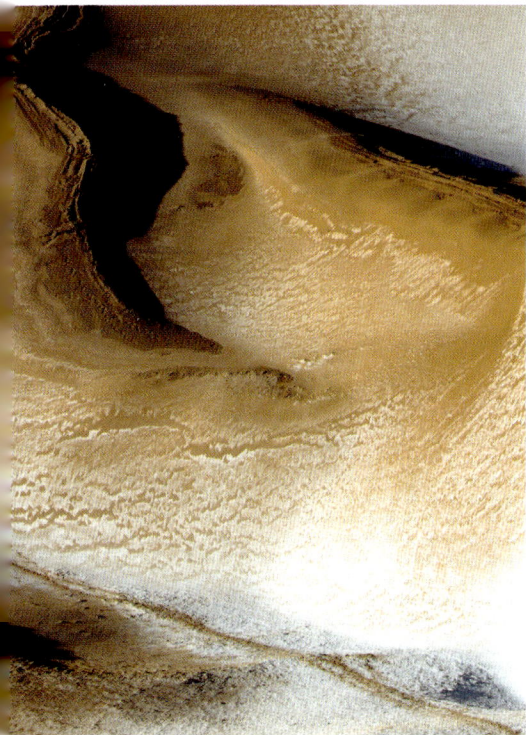

SIMS AZALEA FLOWERS

Wang Qi

A Sims Azalea flower sways in the sun.

Soon summer ends; soon the petals turn to soil.

Only lovers can see this transient moment.

The brevity of life almost robs a face of its redness

Before we find our next incarnation in a fading flower.

We are petals to one another; the prime of our prime

We have bartered. Soon we will become

Soil in the depths of the highlands.

Autumn's breath breathes in before we know it, falling

The flower within, petal by petal, recalling

The furrows of your face.

青海湖或大地之眼

耿占坤

那么多留在沙石中的泪水
忧伤、快乐或者美丽
北风和南风不能夺取动人的饱满
它们不思考不解释，只是蒸发与重聚
在岁月隆起与塌陷的战场上
凝结成我湛蓝色的眼睛。这片高原上
亘古不闭的眼睛，曾经看到天地分离

生命在地上，所以我不能昂起头
我从混沌睁开的眼睛，看到
大地坚硬的细胞如何裂变。收集
昼夜的雨水霜露，以及夏天消融的冰雪
让草原和裸体的鲤鱼在其中生长
让死亡每天在其中复活轮回
我看到女神、雪豹、流血的骏马
踏着冰冷的箭镞和砾石
向远方，迎来羚羊皮包裹的婴儿

神灵在天上，我不敢低垂眼帘
我借助高原的肩膀仰视
看见天河从黑暗世界奔腾而来
未知元素的尘埃卷起圆锥体漩涡
飞溅的浪花陨落，在我黑眼球深处划出
炽热的伤口。然后我看见
峰峦的裙裳染出血色，海鸥化作朝霞
候鸟们用柔软的羽毛托起太阳
为将要启程的儿女举行七月的成年礼

无限事物曾经从我的瞳孔穿越
傲慢与谦卑，喧闹或者沉默的询问
他们不能带走我目光坦荡的秘密
珊瑚和歌谣的馈赠，香柏供奉的轻烟以及
祈祷的青稞，撒在绿度母寂静的田畴
却没有人能够收获我蔚蓝色的果实
于是我转向一个不确定的角度
如此清晰地看见你——诗人的眼睛
透过咸涩水珠的淡淡光明
古老的盐结晶和太阳坚硬的种子

QINGHAI LAKE, EARTH'S EYE

Geng Zhankun

The sediment of tears in stone and gravel,

Redolent of sadness, joy, and a stunning beauty:

Not even the north or the south wind can usurp such moving completeness

Which neither thinks nor explains itself, but simply evaporates and recondenses

Upon this ancient battleground, here elevated, there sunken.

Hence the blue of my eye, an eye that never once shuts close

Upon the highlands, and which has once seen Heaven and Earth part.

Life crawls on Earth, so that I cannot keep my head up.

My eye, born out of chaos, first saw

How the Earth's tough cells divided. Then I gathered

Rain, frost and dew—for days and nights—and the thawing snow of summer, nurturing

The grassland and the naked carps in my bosom, harbouring

The daily cycles of life and death.

I have seen goddesses, snow leopards, and bleeding steeds treading

Among the ice—cold arrowheads fallen on the gravel.

I have seen these horses go far hence, till they were greeted by some gaunt calf antelope from far away.

The deities hover above, so that I cannot lower my lid.

Looking up from the highlands' broad shoulders, I see

The Milky Way's torrents pouring down from the abyss,

A pointed swirl upstirred with the dusts of elements unknown,

With meteors falling from their splashes. Hotly wounded deep

In the black of my eye, I saw

The mountain's hem dyed in blood. The gulls became the dawn light,

Those migratory birds bearing up the sunrise with their soft down,

In a rite of passage for their soon departing offspring.

My pupil once has been a thoroughfare for infinite beings,

But no inquirer, whether proud or humble, loud or quiet, could

Walk away with my candid secrets.

Offerings of coral and chants, cedar—wood yielding its sacrifice of smoke, and

Prayers over highland barley grains are scattered over Tārā's tract of tranquility;

Yet none knew how to harvest my sapphires' fruit.

Desperate for love, I tacked into uncharted territory:

I turned to you—your poet's eye—

Which alone penetrates the glim of my salt teardrops,

Age—old crystals, harsh seeds of the sun.

车过拉脊山

晓音

海拔 3200 米！
这是一个让人仰望的地方

在拉脊山的峰顶
车停了下来
风低低地从脚下吹过
空气中飘浮着云彩和白羊
那一刻，我感觉到了天上

我从来没有想过
自己会有一天
坐着汽车
来到这么高的地方
更没有想过
习惯了朝高处看的我
忽然会站在这样的一个高度上
朝下面看去

而我的下面，是一望无际

CROSSING THE LAJI MOUNTAIN

Xiao Yin

Full 3,200 metres in altitude!
Such a place to look up to.

As the car pulled up on
The Laji Mountain's summit, I felt
A cool wind blowing underfoot, and the air
Bearing flocks of irid clouds and white sheep,
At which moment I felt on heavens.

Never before had I thought of
Some day mounting
To such an altitude
On four wheels.
Neither could I have had imagined
Looking down on the clouds
From on high,
Being so accustomed to humility.

And yet, now all beneath my feet.

在蜜酒般的夏日

徐红

十指相合，
诵经声如水滴滑落。
莲上干净的水，
可以净心。
我闭着眼睛，
听塔尔寺的天籁之音。

在蜜酒般的夏日，
水罐和阴凉是安静的。
温暖的坠落，
不是水鸟，是鱼。
肉身沉重，光沾满皮肤。
青海又美又静。

安静如水，
风吹动尘世的快乐。
走过菩提树下的人，
轻轻地，
合起双手。
要忍住一生的悲伤和欢喜。

MELLIFLUOUS SUMMER

Xu Hong

Ten fingers crossed
Means an overflow of chanting.
Water dripping on the lotus pads
Cleanses the mind.
Two eyes shut,
I open up to the heavenly music wafted
From Ta'er Monastery.

Cool and quiet are the cisterns and shades
In the mellifluous summer,
In whose balmy bosom I fall,
Not like some waterfowl, but like a fish,
Heavy in the body, shimmering in the skin.
Neat and calm is my part of the world.

Calm as a pool of water,
Breeze blows by all the mundane celebrations of good luck.
To pass under the Bodhi Tree,
One must clasp her hands,
Holding within
A lifetime of joys and tears.

沉思的阿尼玛卿雪山

徐燕

为了灵魂的洗礼
有多少生灵从八方聚集此地
站在远处　仰视
虔诚地拜你

立足青藏高原　咫尺之遥
却不敢贸然靠近你
我知自己从尘世中走来
带着一身俗气
怕有辱我此番朝圣的长旅
更怕亵渎你洁净的疆域

让黄河依依不舍
你 6282 米高庞大的身躯
经典的九曲回肠中步步叩首
顾盼成十八个流淌的弯曲

虔诚的大道永无堵塞
朝圣者用身躯竖起路的标记
晨光丈量着长跪者灵魂的深度
贪婪的人欲
烘烤着阿尼玛卿神山的雪线

阿尼玛卿雪山
你可理解我的忧虑
人类污染造孽
真的怕你变瘦变低
甚而蓦然远去
呜呼　倘使你走了
青海湖也会销影匿迹
黄沙将主宰高原晨昏
《格萨尔王》沦为绝唱的哀凄

为了美好的完整
为了圣洁的屹立
我会让一举一动充满警惕
爱护自然　从自己做起

我把这些说给阿尼玛卿
雪山依然禅定无语
坚信　你的不言
乃是对我的默许
啊　方晓天地之间
你万古千秋沉思
当是一尊大神永恒的定力

MEDITATION BY THE AMNYE MACHEN, A SACRED MOUNTAIN OF AMDO

Xu Yan

How many pilgrim souls
Have congregated here from the four winds
Only to behold you from a distance,
For their souls' ablution ?

Though standing on Qinghai—Tibet plateau,
within arm's reach of you,
I dare not go near,
Ashamed in my aura of mundanity—
The imprint of an unexamined life—
Lest I fall short of a pilgrim's ways,
Lest I spoil your holy demesne.

Let the Yellow River's torrents hug your magnificence
—Your bulk of 6,282 metres above the ocean.
May she reverence you every step of the way,
Until her nine longing ogles become
eighteen curvaceous flowing bends.

The path of piety sees no barricades,
Except the pilgrims' bodies lighting our way,
Whose prostrate souls are fathomed by the morning sun

While the human heat of passion scorches
The Amnye Machen's sacred snow line.

Can you understand my angst,
Dear, silent Amnye Machen ?
May we humans cease the mayhem,
Lest you dwarf and dwindle,
Lest you die.
Should that come to pass,
The Qinghai Lake too would be gone, leaving
The highlands to dust from dawn till dark,
And the Epic of King Gesar as their sole swan song.

Thus, for the sake your beauty's integrity,
And your saintly rectitude,
Let me treat Mother Nature with reverence,
And be the change I want to see in the world.

The Amnye Machen echoes my revelation
In still, silent dhyāna,
Rock—solid in her muteness,
A wordless acquiescence.
Only now do I realize, mountain,
That it must be a Deva's everlasting presence that blesses
Your eternal, musing meditation.

油菜花

沙戈

鬓间插花的女儿
花苞里的粉
花瓣中的露
只有鹰才能偷窥

油菜花
只有湖水的篮
和飘动的经幡
才能匹配她的娇艳

——是迅即蔓延的太阳的光斑
承接雷电的温柔的手

一颗紫色的痣
一粒高原上偶尔出现的标点
油菜花：在土里拼命追赶着时间

RAPESEED FLOWERS

Sha Ge

Only a highland eagle's eye can descry

These dewy petals

And the pollinated buds

Worn on a girl's temple.

Only the sapphire lakes of the highlands,

And the Tibetan prayer flags' fluttering

Are in sync with these coy, colourful

Rapeseed flowers.

—Like the speedy spread of sunspots,

Mild hands that receive the thunder,

A mere violet mole they are,

A chance comma arising out of the highlands.

Rapeseed flowers race against time in the dirt.

德令哈

秦巴子

汽车进入德令哈
已经时近黄昏
蓝天白云绿树
和夕光中的街道
看上去很不真实
也许是我久居
灰霾天空之下
也许是我麻木于
都市的喧嚣和
拥挤的人流车流
穿越柴达木
到达德令哈
如同一个俗人
突然到达一座
清幽安静的寺院

DELINGHA CITY

Qin Bazi

It is near the gloaming of day
When I finally drove into Delingha city.
Surreal all seem:
The blue skies, the white clouds, the green trees,
The twilight streets.
A habitual haunter of
The cities' hustles and bustles,
The men-filled streets, the car-filled roads,
Freshly arriving in Delingha
Through the Qaidam Basin,
I suddenly become a layman
Breathing his first breath of
A secluded monastery.

美丽的坎布拉

张烨

坎布拉！美丽的坎布拉！
青海还有何处比你更美？
连歌声也沉默了
连飞鸟也凝定半空了

高山上，香雾拂面
深渊下，绿湖举着十万朵雪浪花
像一面魔镜，制作幻景
多么超然，孤寂在遥远的地方

荒僻使人心静
烦恼的人们只要见到你
灵魂都能长出一棵忘忧草
迎着坎布拉的韵律，曼舞歌唱

谁是第一个见到你的人？
目光轻轻一触，感到你在等我
从我凡尘的瞬间
静候神秘的到来

KANBULA NATIONAL GEOPARK

Zhang Ye

Oh Kanbula, beautiful Kanbula!
Where else can Qinghai boasts finer sights than yours？
—So much so that my singing fails;
And the birds freeze halfway in the sky.

High up on the mountains, fragrant mists fondle my face;
Deep in the abyss, emerald lakes ripple with myriad snow−white splashes;
As if from a magical mirror, mirage appears.
Surreal is the solitude of this secluded clime.

Seclusion makes quiet:
And as the worry−wearied men approach you,
From their souls will sprout blades of bliss,
Singing and dancing to Kanbula's passionate melodies.

Who was it that first saw your true face？
Our eyes meet, and I feel that you have been waiting for eons,
Expecting to surprise the most esoteric of feelings
Out of my mundane moments.

梦与青海

田原

在青海，我做了一个长长的梦
梦见一群巨大的秃鹰
钩状的尖喙上沾满人血
翅膀上驮着死者的魂灵
它们在半空中盘旋、盘旋
仿佛迷失在飞往天国的路上

梦中的湖水淹没天空的倒影
淹不死的是漂流在湖底的云朵
和秃鹰的滑翔以及鸟声的悠扬
寸草不生的远山似乎还在疯长
那绵延的荒凉
加剧着我内心的孤独感

我像一个缺乏虔诚的信徒
在塔尔寺前的菩提树下
沐浴着被它的叶片剪碎的阳光
那远道而来衣衫褴褛、额头叩响大地的膜拜者
他们让我身上的文明荡然无存

神龛里袅袅升天的白烟
如同一句忌讳说破的箴言
绿松石里藏满了时间的秘密
胸前佩戴着牦牛骨和藏羚羊角首饰的和尚
他那刚毅的目光
看上去显得神圣而不可侵犯

在草原上飘动的经幡是另一种旗帜
它昭示活着的平凡和死亡的伟大
爬出洞口觅食的香鼬把阳光藏入皮毛
猞猁狲尖锐的目光让人畏惧
这一切或许都跟高原有关

三江之源的青海离天堂很近
它让我的梦充满色彩与神奇
包括它拥抱的雪山
和那雪山立足的荒原

I DREAMED A DREAM

Tian Yuan

In Qinghai, I dreamed a long, long dream
Of a large pack of vultures,
Acqualine beaks that dripped with human
blood,
Who bore departed human spirits on their
wingspans,
Hovering, hovering in the middle of the air,
As if lost on the way to the Kingdom of
Heaven.

In my dream, the sky's reflection was
submerged by the lake,
But the clouds at the bottom did not drown,
Nor did the gliding of the vultures or the
melody of birdsong.
The distant barren mountains still were
growing.
A bleakness spread on all four sides, aggrieving
The forlorn heart within.

A pilgrim lukewarm in piety, I was basking
beneath
A Bodhi Tree at Ta'er Monastery
In the sunlight shredded by the foliage,
When the tattered homage of kumbum
devotees from afar
Put my genteel manners to shame.

The white wisps of smoke coming from the
tabernacles
Was an esoteric mantra too deep to construe.
The torquoise stones smacked of the secret of
the eons.
With dangling amulets of yak's bone and
Tibetan antelope's horn,
And a stern, stalwart countenance,
That monk over there looked literally
incorruptible.

The grassland's prayer flags seemed
otherworldly banners,
Symbols of life's triviality and death's triumph.
The mountain weasels, foraging outside their
burrows, basked their furry lengths in the sun;
The Tibetan lynxes had the most intimidating
stares ever—
All were tempered by the highland clime.

Qinghai, with its headwaters of three giant
rivers, is closest to heaven;
It dazzles my dreams with iridescence and awe,
Illumined and inspired by the embraces of
snow mountains,
And the majestic barrens on which they stand.

河源月

白渔

大草原白天牧羊
夜晚牧月亮

一群群
在鄂陵、扎陵湖嬉戏
在星宿海徜徉
悬在天空
浮在湖面
隐现草莽
一千个月亮辉煌山川
也把我心中的阴影照亮

河源，月之故乡
引出我多少遐想
哦哦！这里
最缺少人烟

最不缺光亮
最富有清爽……

MOONLIGHT AT THE HEADWATERS

Bai Yu

In the vast grassland graze the flocks by day,
And the moon by night.

Flocks frolick
By the sister lakes of Zhaling and Eling.
They rove the sea of the constellations
Pendent in the sky,
Suspended on the lake,
And elusive in the wild.
A thousand moons light up the nooks and crannies of the landscape.
They also light up those of my heart.

Oh, the headwaters, land of the rising moon—
What fancies you have evoked in me!
Oh, you—a territory
Most lacking in human habitation,
Least wanting in light,
And most redolent of a brisk liveliness...

坎布拉之忆

姚辉

我的沉默是否能比初秋的正午更为锐利？
坎布拉　当你的翅翼开始旋转
我　是否还能在你莽阔的飞翔中
接近　种种陈旧的眷顾与怀念？

坎布拉　我已从风声之刃上划过
我划过　我的路途　代表了
多少艰辛而新颖的灿烂

我还将从怎样的眺望里归来？
天色在典籍之外　我在沙砾之外
峰峦上　鸟唱反复消失
你的身影　带来前所未有的晕眩……

而沧桑依旧沉寂
像堆积年年的所有喧哗　坎布拉
你比我坚守一生的梦想　更为遥远

IN MEMORY OF KANBULA NATIONAL GEOPARK

Yao Hui

Is my silence more cutting than the heat of an early autumn midday ?

For all your circular wing–flappings, Kanbula,

Will I still penetrate to my manifold nostalgia

Across your long–distanced, full–fledged flight ?

I glided along a whistling blade of wind towards you：

And the distance I have covered

Represents I do not know how many miles of trials and tribulations.

I will be back to normal from what manner of far–gazing ?

With the skies beyond the chronicles' bounds, and me out of reach by the drift sands,

Atop the peaks and folds birds warble and cry in polyphony；

Your presence puts on a dizziness I have never felt before...

Experience, like the white noise stored up over the years,

Remains silent. Kanbula, you are far more out–of–the–way

Than all my life's work and aspirations.

门源百里花海之美

荣荣

这样的美是有呼吸的
微风里她们小小的胸脯起伏

这样的美是有灵魂的
她们油亮的祷词让群山肃穆

这样的美有着庄重的仪式感
亿万朵鲜花　每一朵都藏起意志
为暖过来的春天　辅就百里黄金花垫

这样的美可以一再地渲染
但我屏气敛息　在尘世太久了
随意的夸赞也会是喧哗

我将双手比画成一张大弓
我的虚空之击　惊起一群幸福的蜜蜂

100 MILES OF RAPESEED FLOWERS SEA IN MENYUAN, QINGHAI

Rong Rong

Some beauty, that breathes!
Tiny bosoms heaving in the breeze.

Some beauty, that isn't soulless!
—Whose glistening prayers put the mountains in awe.

Some beauty, of such ceremonial dignity,
That billions of flowers uniformly hide their intent—
To pave a hundred-mile golden carpet for the
thawing spring.

Some beauty, about which I can go on and on—
But now I hold my tongue, for in this mundane
world of ours,
Even the most casual remark is too boisterous to be true.

Elated by such beauty, I stretch my arms in a gesture
of triumph
To the slight surprise of the nectared bees.

西宁诗章

谭五昌

西宁，你的命名在汉语的园地
如格桑花般散发出阴性的吉祥之美

静静远眺辽阔的北国与南疆
你是一座属于西部的宁静的城

在炎炎七月，无边的清凉让你成为一所避暑胜地
但其实你的居民们终年内心都怀揣一团火苗

到处是清洁的街道、清真风味小吃和淳朴的笑脸
西宁的女子有着本土诗人们一样脱俗的美与热情

至今我到过五次西宁，或逗留或途经
与梦境般的西宁结下了五次美丽的缘分

XINING CANTO

Tan Wuchang

Xining: your nomenclature exudes

A propitious feminine beauty like the Tibetan Sims Azalea flower.

Coolly looking over her northern climes and southern bounds,

You truly belong to China's peaceful west.

Summer's height elsewhere makes you a haven of boundless delight,

But your men and women are afire all year round.

Spotless streets everywhere, where savoury Halal comes bite-sized, where artless smiles come free

of charge—

Where local women, like the local poets, parade a passion too beautiful to be deemed earthly—

I have been to Xining five times, either for sojourn or for transit,

And each time struck up a serendipitous sensation.

西宁晚风

杨然

没想到在赤裸山原怀抱
西宁是这样秀丽清爽
天空比所有城市更高更广
最美是夏夜吹来徐徐晚风

拥有高原壮丽的日照
不影响绿荫掐熄烈烈火苗
走进树影，顿时沉浸惬意清凉
身在闹市也会显得轻轻飘飘

忽然你说：我有些冷了
这么热的天呵，晚风在制造冰窖
所有城市都在埋怨酷暑难熬
西宁相告：别忘了带上秋装一套

夜空洗得更深更蓝
预示着明日依然气温火爆
但不要紧，西宁有的是解渴之道
雪在杯中飞舞，水在零度燃烧

城市的高楼总是一样的
只有晚风不同，看谁把谁吹倒
注定是高原的大美之城
狂热在西宁永远逃票

注定是高原的大爱之城
最爱是诗歌的精神普照
晚风善解诗人无边情怀
近有吉狄马加，远有圣者昌耀

EVENING BREEZE IN XINING

Yang Ran

Never have I imagined such beauty to belong
to her.
Nestled in the naked mountains' cool embraces,
Xining boasts a sky-dome more encompassing
than that of most cities',
And the best summer evening breeze that ever
blows.

A most splendid highland sun
Does not keep the green shades from quenching
the people's heart-fires.
I walk under a tree, and a cool comfort
Levitates me from the urban stew.

And you say: "Well, it is getting cold—"
Sure. Despite the swelter elsewhere,
Here the evening breeze is blowing rife,
Carving out an ice-dome while all other cities
complain of heat.
"Bring your own jacket," Xining reminds us
gently.

Tonight, the azurean wash of the sky
Forecasts even more intense heatwaves tomorrow.
Do not worry, though: Xining never runs out of
solutions.
Here, beer mugs brim with snowy foams, and
water flames
Even at zero degree Celcius.

Here, the cityscape, uniform in height,
Is confronted with jagged breeze. Who will win ?
Destined to become the highlands' jewel,
Xining escapes with fashion.

Destined to become the highlands' Capital of
Love,
Xining cherishes a poet's universal sentiments,
As the evening breeze tunes in on the messages
Of the poet Jidi Majia, and the friars out in the
mountains.

青海湖畔

杨梓

越过金黄色的油菜花
我看见了青海湖
一望无际的湛蓝令人眩晕
更不敢面对
仿佛觉得自己内心的阴影
会被湖光照亮

十万只候鸟在湖上盘旋
十万条湟鱼在湖里游荡
我捧起湖水尝了一口
这咸涩的大地之泪啊
一浪一浪地把沙子推到岸边
我成了其中的一粒

COMPOSED BY THE QINGHAI LAKE

Yang Zi

Crossing a golden rapesseed field, I see
The Qinghai Lake glittering in a sapphiric blue,
Vast, dazzling to the eye.
I dare not greet it face-to-face,
Lest my heart's shadows
Be unearthed by such blinding light.

Seeing a bevy of migratory birds hovering over the lake,
And a school of naked carps roaming about its vast expanse,
I cup a handful of water and taste
The briny tears of the highlands, wreathing
Waves upon waves of sand around the brim,
Myself a tiny grain among the many.

塔尔寺一把小红伞

叶延滨

雨后的塔尔寺是打开闸口的小河
那么多的人头攒动
路看不见
路在人头起伏的波浪上面
上面，上面
一把导游姑娘的小红伞

雨后的塔尔寺是云和雾的家园
那么多的眼光浮动
菩萨看不见
菩萨在香烟缭绕的仙境上面
上面，上面
一把虔诚高举的小红伞

雨后的塔尔寺是展开的唐卡画卷
那么多的心愿转动
那么多的转经筒
转经筒上面还有飘动的经幡上面
上面，上面
一把引领我游历的小红伞

神秘的塔尔寺雨后更加地神秘莫测
塔尔寺在今天就是引领我的小红伞……

LITTLE RED UMBRELLA AT TA'ER MONASTERY

Ye Yanbing

The monastery after the rain is like a sluicing river,
Navigated by the a fleet of bobbing heads, crowding
Over the pilgrims' path now unseen
Except over the waves of tourists—
Over... over...
Over a little red umbrella in a girl tour guide's hand.

The monastery after rain is home to clouds of mist,
Haunted by so many beams of eyes, floating
With the Bodhisattvas unseen—
Bodhisattvas sitting in fairyland—
Up... up...
Up on the little red umbrella in the pious, lofty hand.

The monastery after rain is like a thangka unfurled,
With countless prayer wheels swirling and hovering
—So many prayer wheels gyrating,
Topped by prayer flags fluttering—
Topped... Topped...
Topped by the little red umbrella guiding me across the holy land.

A mysterious shrine, mistier than the rain,
Ta'er Monastery is the little red umbrella that makes my day...

在圣湖里濯洗灵魂

亚楠

这圣洁之水与阳光一起让
我们的信仰闪耀着光芒
没有人读懂，此刻一滴水的内心
充满神圣和庄严

红尘已经把我们氧化
锈迹斑斑，腐朽淹没了灵魂

在世俗里沉浮，混沌却又神机妙算
把自己的影子装饰成图腾
顶礼膜拜，这是每天都能看到的情景

或者用一只猥琐的眼在风雨
飘摇的世界之外看春天不再迷茫

而大地是慈祥的
这一汪圣水注定会成为我们
心灵最后栖息的地方

THE SOUL'S ABLUTION IN THE HOLY LAKE

Ya Nan

Sparkling in the sun, the holy water
Glorifies our faith through its glitters.
Yet no one can read in a water drop
Its sacred majesty.

Oxydized in the human world, we are
Souls rusted all over.

Through mundane, murky calculations
We have totemized our self−images
Which we worship constantly. We see
But our selves daily, and we deem this normal.

—Until, through sick eyes, we see
Some certainty of the spring blooming outside our shabby world.

Mother Earth is generous after all,
Offering us this sacred pond as
Our last spiritual resort.

天下黄河贵德清

朱剑

把眼前这条河流
叫作黄河
实在叫不出口

我愿意我
还有其他中国诗人
在河边拍照抽烟聊天
探讨她何时何地变黄变浊之时
就像谈论邻居家一个学坏的孩子
回忆起她儿时的可爱天真
顺口叫出了她的小名

我还羡慕同车而来
又早早离开的外国同行
他们中一定有这么一位
对它一无所知也不关心
在一个陌生的地方看到
并爱上这条清澈的河流
只因美丽

GUIDE IS AT THE LIMPIDEST OF THE YELLOW RIVER

Zhu Jian

How can I call
This glassy stream stretching before me
The Yellow River？

I had rather that I,
With my fellow Chinese poets,
(Chatting and snapping photos on her bank,
While occasionally taking a smoke,)
Had discussed when and where she had turned yellow,
Like speaking of a neighbour's child gone astray in life,
And, recalling that she too had been lovely and innocent,
Uttered her pet name out of love.

How I admire my international colleagues
Who had come here by car for just a brief sojourn,
Among whom there must have been one
Who neither had known nor thought much of the river,
But somehow had fallen in love at once
With this limpid, babbling brook
For its stunning beauty.

青海，青海

潘红莉

它高于我生命中所有的梦境　青海
它让我的奢望升高更为广阔
那么无限　取之心的索求
干净悠远　在青草之上的蔚蓝

青海　将画布打开马儿在白云下漫步
湖天一色　深邃的静美绝世的
孤中的不动　青海湖
那属于一个人最为盛世的平静

这只属于天地的神域
一点点的虚伪都是亵渎
哪里都是合适的安顿浑然天成
露水在花之上　生灵的隐性
青海　这里从没有偏爱的破译
它在它不在就是无就是如愿
无法形容的靠近却那么旷达

八方的静美　青海
真正的还给这世界的美　独一的无瑕
这里不飞翔也高　仿佛世界的清晨都在这里
凝固的安宁透彻和灵魂一体

QINGHAI, QINGHAI

Pan Hongli

Loftier than my dreamland, Qinghai taught me
To wish for higher things of the mind.
Expansive, genuine, pristine and faraway,
It is an emerald grassland under the blue sky.

A canvas of horses sauntering beneath the clouds,
Qinghai is home to blue gems of lakes mirroring the
skies.
An esoteric still life of stunning serenity,
The pacific Qinghai Lake belongs wholly to me in its
seclusion.

Any white of falsehood would be sacrilege
To this god-given terrain, nature's true bequest,
Where everything fits snugly in its place,
Such as the dew-moistened flowers, deep-meaning
symbols of creation.
There is no synonym of "prejudice" or "illusion" here,
Where the world is simply at one with its being:
The nearer it approaches, the more profound it is.

Emanating the blessings of peace to all four winds,
Qinghai rewards all under heaven with its unique
charms.
It is where you can get "high" (in both senses of the
word) without flying;
It is the dawn of the world, one with its Soul and at
peace.

那一晚，我是你
——致青海湖
孙萌

你说你想成为阿喀琉斯成为赫克托耳
成为英雄成为格萨尔
你说其实今晚你只想成为一条鱼

夜晚用树汲取正午的强光
让日神与月神靠到最近
你拥抱我，像揽起一面虚空的镜子
一颗蓝色的星里，一万颗星闪耀
一朵云里，一万朵云飘浮
我身上的小精灵打开眼眸
深渊的光辉，泪的晶体
一片片飘落的树叶刻上玉的质地梦的肌理
风与尘埃一起飞升，流过无数纪元
静卧的那片蓝不过是神灵的衣钵
我们还要执拗地在你我之间找到灵魂

今晚，所有忧郁的嘴都在呼喊
今晚，所有孤独的脸都在海上哭

无穷无尽无边无际的青海湖
把我们的昨天拿走
又把酒、盐、泪和血洒进我们的今天、明天

QINGHAI LAKE，I BECAME YOU THAT NIGHT

Sun Meng

You say that you want to become Achilles, become Hector, become Hero,

become King Gesar—

You say you only want to become a fish tonight.

The night consumes the dazzling sun through the trees' photosynthesis,

Wedding the sun to the moon deities.

You embrace me as if I am an empty mirror.

The myriad stars are shining in the eyes of the blue planet;

The myriad wisps of clouds are skidding in the bosom of a giant wisp.

The infant sprite in me opens its eyes to

Your abysmal light, a crystal of tear.

The fallen leaves are engraved with the patterns of jade and the texture of dreams.

The wind of karma blows the specks of sentient beings and that goes on for eons.

Though your blue repose is the true bequest of the deities,

We still must struggle to find our souls in our daily transactions.

Every melancholic mouth must howl tonight;

Every forlorn face must cry at sea.

Qinghai Lake—infinite and boundless—

You have made your rightful claim of our yesterdays,

And you will dash your wine, you salt, you blood, and your tears into our todays and tomorrows.

我们本该有三个孩子

从容

老大叫谷雨，她在春天发芽在夏天的泥淖里枯黄
老二叫白露，她被风轮吸引，一个趔趄，
被穿白大褂的人扔进生锈的铁桶　只活了39天

老三叫小雪，她无法被更苍凉的子宫孕育
我无数次见过她们的眼睛⋯⋯
比辽阔的黑暗大海还要深陷于无底的黑暗
比太阳的目光更尖锐地在夜晚刺痛我的太阳穴、承泣穴、大椎穴、劳宫穴与丹田

有时她们用会哭的眼睛在房顶整夜地盘旋
我屏息谛听，独自在寒夜三更披衣、点灯、燃香、诵经
领受他们对任督二脉和太阳穴以及所有穴位的突袭和击打
我要窒息，我要疼痛，我要头悬梁锥刺股
我要让头和身体的每一毫米在有生之年被她们银针一样的眼睛扎满、再扎满
我要扎满所有穴位，替她们受过！

WE ONCE HAD THREE CHILDREN

Cong Rong

Our oldest was named Gu Yu (Grain Rain). She budded in the spring and turned sallow in the summer's sludge.

Our second was named Bai Lu (White Dew). Spellbound by a whirl of wind, she stumbled badly, was Thrown by someone wearing a lab coat into a rusty bucket. She lived only 39 days.

Our youngest was named Xiao Xue (Minor Snow). She could not be nurtured by a colder womb.

Many times I have gazed at their eyes,

Darker than the boundless, benighted ocean,

More acute than the sharp stings of the sun. At night they pierced the acupuncture points of my body:

Greater Yang (Taiyang), Big Vertebra (Dazhui), Palace of Toil (Laogong), Field of Elixir (Dantian).

Sometimes with weeping eyes they would hover above my roof for nights—during which time I held my breath and listened. I would wake up alone in the third watch of the night, put on my clothes, light a candle, burn a incense stick, and recite the sutras,

Then they would send down their blessings by ramming and pounding my Conception (Ren) and my Governor (Du) vessels as well as my Great Yang and so on.

I almost asphyxiated. Yet I wanted that pain to go on. I wanted those trials and tribulations.

I wanted every inch of my head and my body within my lifetime to bristle with the silver needles of their stares over and over again.

I wanted all my acupuncture points pierced, so as to pardon their sins on my children's behalf.

后来，在一个格桑花开的下午
她们再也没有触碰我的太阳穴、承泣穴、大椎穴、劳宫穴与丹田
她们离开了我的身体，她们去了哪儿
她们无视我、遗忘我了吗？
我想要再一次疼痛！我要见她们！

在青海湖边，我看见了
她们有高原女孩的眼睛，她们站在嘛呢石堆，为我添加了一块嘛呢石
她们在路边种下一排格桑花，等我经过时戴在我发白的鬓角
她们用眼睛长久地凝视我，凝视我的皱纹
凝视我的太阳穴、承泣穴、大椎穴、劳宫穴与丹田
直到我们都微笑着泪眼婆娑

就这样，我在她们的目光中融化
就这样，融化成为了她们的母亲

痛苦带领我们遇见最美的事物

Later on, in a blooming afternoon of Sims Azalea,

They ceased touching me. They stopped poking at me in the Great Yang, Tear Container (Chengqi), Big

Vertebra, Palace of Toil, and Field of Elixir.

They had left my body—but for where ?

Had they forgotten me ? Perhaps they had thrown me into a sea of oblivion ?

No way. I needed that pain once more. I needed to see my daughters!

And I saw them. I saw them

Standing by the Qinghai Lake. I saw their highland ladies' eyes. I saw them beside a Mani cairn, adding

one more piece to the pile just for my sake.

They planted by the wayside a row of Sims Azalea, and put one on my temple when I passed them.

They gazed long at me, at my face full of wrinkles.

They gazed at my Great Yang, at my Container of Tears, my Big Vertebra, my Elixir Field—

Until the four of us broke into tears of gratitude.

So be it—let me melt into the light of their eyes.

So be it—let me melt into their mother.

This is what good painful experiences can bring about!

少女 · 仓央嘉措，与青海湖

唐德亮

暮风，擦暗了天空
苍茫的湖，沉醉于
它自己的深邃丰腴和辽阔
仓央嘉措。这位从布达拉宫
押解过来的情圣。携着歌，诗，雪风
揣着满腔的悲愁痛苦
在寂静的青海湖之夜
与一位神秘的少女相遇

这是人与神的相遇
是灵与肉的相遇
是痛苦与幸福的相遇
是冬天与春天的相遇

于是一个传说在青海湖诞生
不朽的诗篇在青海湖诞生
天地之间　不见了官吏与士卒
只剩下仓央嘉措，少女
和他们美丽浪漫的身影
迷人的诗篇，在高原
流传　一代，一代
又一代……

QINGHAI LAKE, AND THE 6TH DALAI LAMA IN LOVE

Tang Deliang

Evening breeze upon the firmament dull—
The immensity of the lake is immersed
In its unfathomable depth, buxomness, and breadth.
Tsangyang Gyatso, Tibet's fabled Lama in love,
Is escorted from his palace, the Potala,
Holding to his songs and his poetry in the bitterness
of the blizzard
Upstirred in his melancholy bosom.
He is on his way to tryst with a mysterious girl
In the night's repose by the Qinghai Lake.

An overlap of the human with the divine, it is
A exchange between body and spirit—
The pangs of remorse intermingled with pleasure,
And the sight of the pent-up winter heralding the
forthcoming spring.

Hence the birth of a legend by the lake,
The beginning of an immortal tale along its banks,
Where the Lama's host and his entourage are all gone,
And only he remains, her hand in his,
The shadow of a romance looming.
Later on, down the generations,
On the sacred highlands would pass
His songs, and well
Into the future.

在贵德

语伞

黄河之外的激动，并非次要
在贵德国家地质公园，岩石的褶皱
如书籍重叠。一座陡峭的图书馆
它赤壁丹崖的智慧，不得不俯视
一个图书馆管理员的渺小和愚笨

我突然想去分清石头与泥土的关系
像去分清插图和空缺，文言和白话
字体和尘埃的关系
像去分清父母、我和钟摆的声部
作者：大自然；编辑：岁月

读者：我，内心虚空的行者
在越来越低的天空下，显得无所适从
这时，高原上的云朵
像亲爱的人，走过来，填空

WHERE THE YELLOW RIVER GETS COOL AND CLEAR

Yu San

It is not that I am not interested in the Yellow River,

But in Guide National Greopark, creases in the rocks

Are like tomes piled up on top of one another within the precipitous library walls

Housing the red−cliffs stuffed with wisdom. So I cannot help looking down

On the parochial naivete of human librarians.

All of a sudden, I feel an irresistible urge to tell stone and the sludge apart,

As I would normally do between illustrations and the white space on a page, between formal diction and

colloquial;

Between the telling fonts and some paltry specks of dust;

Just as I must tell my two parents apart, must tell my vocal line from the clock's striking in the grand

symphony of life.

All I have learned is this: that it is Mother Nature who authored all of creation, but it is time who puts the

notes on the margins.

Reader: I, an empty−hearted seeker,

Am more than ever at a loss under the looming sky,

When suddenly some highland clouds,

Like a lover, drift over and fill in the blank for me.

青海云

晴朗李寒

只有神的居所，才能游牧着这样的云朵。
这青海之云，庞大的家族，自由的部落，
白与美，是他们共同的姓氏。
他们在辽远的天际，草原青绿的尽头，
灰色的群山之上，
悠游，放荡，这里有足够的空间
供他们任性地奔跑，放任地追逐，激情地交媾，
他们在无边的蔚蓝色天空的舞台上，
演化出无穷的大剧。
这些云的兵团在青海的上空集结，
它们将闪电、霹雳、雨水，
深藏于绵绵的柔絮之中，
默默地从大地上喷涌而出。
只有在青海，这些云才白得这样恣肆，
浓得如此大胆。
我坚信，它们是被众神引领的，
除此外，没有其他的解释。

QINGHAI CLOUDS

Qinglang Lihan

Only at the abode of deities can such flowery
clouds be grazing carelessly—
These clouds of Qinghai, in a giant family, a clan
celebrating freedom,
Boast White and Beautiful as their surnames.
Along the dim skyline, beyond the verdant
grassland, upon the gray mountain ridges,
The clouds roam and revel, rejoicing in their ample
realm
And cavorting, pursuing passionate intercourse
—To put on a play of fickle variation and change
Upon the azurean stage of the sky.
The battalion of clouds are here assembled
With an arsenal of lightening, thunderbolt and rain
under their cottony softness,
Spurting out silently upon the land.
It is only here in Qinghai that they will parade their
whiteness in such abandon, and their thickness with
such audacity,
I do believe that they are heavenly inspired.
For no other theory seems to suffice.

在格尔木

马非

在格尔木街头
当我提及昆仑山
你手指远处
一抹朦胧的山脉
告诉我：
"那就是"

我没有惊讶
我已经习惯于
伟大的事物出现时
那种稀松平常的
静悄悄的方式

脚踩肉垫
猫步而来

GOLMUD

Ma Fei

In the streets of Golmud,
Should I bring up the Kunlun Mountains,
You would simply point
To a misty wash of mountains
And say,
"Over there."

No surprise on my part—
Me so accustomed
To the mute inglorious manner
Greatness slips in
Through the backdoor,

Walking on fleshy pads,
In feline steps.

旅行的回忆

桑克

水里长了很多藻，
对岸树丛中的苏制飞机，
南禅寺，天光，
交谈在表面和深处。

左派和右派，
也不那么清晰了，
如同贵德青碧色的水，
从哪里开始浑浊的？

不恰当的联想，
大着胆的朗诵，
都会吸引客气的体温，
书和签名哪一个更沉？

测试着自己的反应，
湖水与礼帽；
地面的光反映到天上，
反而掩护了群星。

换乘电瓶车，
在斑斓的石头之间。
我戴着黑色的兜帽，
我是摄魂怪。

看得见的别扭，
看不见的秘密，
事前事后才能显现自己的花纹，
而我尽可能抱着青灰色的镇静。

左边一个河谷，
两只飞得极低的鹰几与巴士相平，
路下面又是山谷，
远处的山犹如摞在一起的石饼。

我能调解谁的分歧？
是人非要与自然对应。
我喜欢水果胜过蜜饯，
我喜欢好听的声音胜过了脸蛋。

酥油花融化的部分
也能追求打折的真理；
而博物馆的惊奇并置
也就是不惊奇。

惊奇过度了
才会产生欲。
而风景是数码照相机的女儿，
油菜花的花裙。

水井巷是生活的，
高原反应与变红变黑的肤色，
是一种深度翻译，
从矛盾之中缓和下来。

TRAVEL SNAPSHOTS

Sang Ke

The blooming algae in a pond—
The foliage around a Soviet Air Force wreckage
across the water—
A Zen Monastery, a spot of skylight—
Conversations sifting through the layers.

Left or right ?
It is not so clear-cut.
From what point on
Does the Yellow River turn turbid ?

Bizarre imagery—
Bravadoes of eloquence—
All attract lukewarm compliments.
But which has more weight ? A book or its author ?

The lake and a dress hat
Test my reflexes.
The sky mirroring the sheen of the land
Puts the stars under cover.

I hop on an electromobile
Skipping nimbly among the stones,
And pull my hood over my head
—A soul vampire am I.

Seen awkwardness
And unseen mystery
Only show their true colours postmortem.
For now I must cling on to my ash gray coolness.

A river valley on the left.
Two eagles flying at the bus's height.
Another valley beneath the road
Extends to the piles of stone discuses of mountains.

I must mediate the differences—between whom ?
—If only man didn't wage war on nature in the
first place.
I prefer fresh fruit to candied ones—
I like pleasing noises better than made-up faces.

Tibetan butter flowers' melted petals
Can still attain enlgihtenment at a discount;
Strange juxtapositions in the museum
Surprise me not.

Excessive wonder leads to Lust.
Landscape is the digital camera's daughter
And the rapeseed flowers' hemline.

Water Well Alley is packed with life:
Altitude sickness and the bloodred faces
Are its literary translation
Into where duality subsides.

青海湖

马海轶

从望得见青海湖的那刻起
我就想着青海湖的下面
一群一群的鱼
在一群一群的鱼下面
还应有一个湖
和青海湖一般的大，一般的蓝
或者更大，更蓝

从到想这另一个湖的那刻起
我就爱上了它
我屏住呼吸
俯视黑沉沉的湖面
鱼翅在我的上面
哧剌剌飞过
有时从青海湖的水面上
透下一丝微弱的光亮
使我始终能意识到方向

QINGHAI LAKE

Ma Haiyi

Ever since I was able to behold the Qinghai Lake from the
distance
Did I imagine
Shoals of fish underneath this beautiful lake.
And further down beneath these throngs
There is yet another mysterious lake—
Of the same breadth, and the same blue,
If not even bigger and bluer.

Ever since the thought of this second lake crossed my mind
Did I fall in love with its faithful reflection of the first.
So I held my gasping breath,
Looking over its oppressively dark mirror—
Fish fins fly overhead
In a loud, boisterous racket
While the sun shines over the Qinghai Lake,
Sometimes a feeble glimmer sometimes,
And gently lighting my groping way.

银河

苇欢

车入乌兰县
驶过连绵的油菜花田
和巨大的风车群
经过一片空旷的原野
牛羊已看不见
眼前的画面突然收窄
窄成一道
狭长的银线
我心知那是茶卡盐湖
脱口而出的
却是另外两个字
"银河"

THE GALAXY

Wei Huan

As we drove slowly into Ulan County
Through an endless expanse of bloooming rapeseed
flowers
And a constellation of wind turbines—
As we drove through a vast field of sparse growth,
Where the vegetating livestock could be seen no
more—
All of a sudden, the panorama before us narrowed:
It homed in on
A slender silver thread,
Which I knew at once to be Chaka Salt Lake.
Yet it was something else that I blurted out,
An outlandish word for an outlandish sight:
I blurted out "Galaxy".

站在青海湖边看青海湖

杨森君

我看见——
湖水在天空中漂移

这不是我的错觉
事实可能本来如此

我相信有人
也会这样觉得

只是
他没有说出来

QINGHAI LAKE LOOK OUT

Yang Senjun

Perhaps it is not a hallucination,

But some rock−solid truth that I see.

Before my incredulous eyes,

A watery lake is skidding sideways in the sky.

I suppose I am not the only one

Who sees and thinks this way,

But only I have the audacity to say it,

While others don't.

青色的海

丫丫

青色的海，已被我们盛入酒杯
诗歌是一粒致幻剂
在舌尖，随便就能开出咸湿的蓝色小花

来，干杯——干杯
剪掉杯底激起的浪花
用眼睛磨成剪子

来，干杯——
咸水撞击咸水
脆响

玻璃裹着的心碰着心
这其间美妙的延时
养育诗意

对着青海湖朗诵。今夜
打破湖面，打破夜穹
打破杯子

在破碎中，重现一个新的整体

THE ETYMOLOGY OF QINGHAI LAKE

Ya Ya

A "blue sea" it denotes, poured into the poet's cup,

A poet composing verses as if on a hallucinogen,

From whose tongue tip spurt the water splashes like damp, saline little blue flowers.

Come! let us dry our cups—cheers!

Drain your cup to the bottom of any liquid

With scissors of your own eyes' making.

Come, let us dry our cups,

Where briny water splashes against itself

With such brisk clinks!

Between two fragile souls colliding with one another

In dreamy slow motion,

Poetry is fermented.

Reciting my verses to the Qinghai Lake,

Tonight my voice will cut through its airy blue surface and the night firmament

As it does my wine cup, and

From the shatters derive a brand-new whole.

高原

刘大伟

从海洋中走出的蓝
被长久地，搁置在高大陆的顶端
平静，辽阔，风寒

时光很慢，你还不来
雪花已变作雨，汇成世间所有的
河流，又凝滞为疑惑的冰面

在不断倾斜的生命里，它小心翼翼地
呜咽，借一群野驴咆哮
却不忍耗尽，奔向你的势能

所有的词语已回到石头，成为真言
现在，高原只剩下轻轻诵经的幡
和一大片无人照看的蔚蓝

THE TABLELAND

Liu Dawei

The blue of the lake was stranded from its home in the
ocean.
Tectonic movements have left it suspended atop the
tableland,
Weathering the cold blasts with a body bleak and broad.

Time edges its way slowly, and your arriving footsteps are
even more sluggish.
Snowflakes melted as rain, as a confluence of
All the world's rivers, and froze again on the ice-clad
ground.

In the ever precarious life of man, water gurgles
Timidly, reincarnating as the braying of the wild donkeys,
Yet still saving momentum as it rushes towards you.

Every word in the language was returned to the stones as
some mantra,
Leaving the highlands with nothing but prayer flags
Chanting next to an untended spread of sapphire.

克鲁克湖

安琪

从蓝色到蓝色
克鲁克湖
你浇灌火辣的蓝色

游船劈开的波浪，白纸一样翻滚
你寂寞的湖畔寂寞星散的祁连石
挤满哭泣和微笑的皱纹

那在黄昏迅速变凉的克鲁克湖
鸟回到它的天堂
鱼回到它的故乡
芦苇丛中
数不尽的黑暗在舞蹈

行吟歌者跋涉千山来到这里
他弹，他唱
密集的白云在天上微微抖动
白云忙于自生
白云忙于自灭

你行吟歌者的低沉还在我的耳畔徘徊
告诉我，克鲁克湖
他是否传染了你又咸又淡的悲伤？

LAKE HURLEG

An Qi

Shimmering from emerald to turquoise:
Oh Lake Hurleg,
You indeed are an influencer of fiery blue.

Your waves cleft by the boat bloom like white paper flowers;
Your lonely banks are studded with stones of grotesque shapes,
And crowded with cries and wrinkled smiles.

Your lakewater cools quickly in the bleak dust, sending
Birds back to their safe haven, driving
The fish back to their homelike habitat in your bosom.
In the reed marsh by your banks, there are dancing
Endless figures under the camouflage of darkness.

A troubadour ventured here across a thousand mountains,
Singing and harping along the way,
Sending slight thrills through the clustered white clouds
Now busy blooming,
Now busy dying.

Your rich baritone voice still lingers in my ear,
So tell me, Lake Hurleg (now sweet, now salty),
Is our bard affected with your sadness of ambivalent taste ?

车过贵南草原

杨廷成

我走遍青海大地
只为期待这一季青稞的成熟

三月雨从辽远的天空中飘洒
五月花在广阔的大地上盛开
才有了眼前这风吹麦浪的庄稼

雪峰守望着你圣洁的灵魂
山风劲吹着你坦荡的胸襟

这一垄又一垄金黄的麦地
阳光下每一株穗子低垂感恩的头颅
月色里每一支麦芒挑着深情的泪珠

十万亩青稞为这个季节尽情舞蹈
十万盏酒杯为这个良宵肆意欢呼
今夜草原无眠
这照亮了半个天空的篝火
将燃烧起风暴般掠过旷野的酒歌

CROSSING THE GUINAN GRASSLAND

Yang Tingcheng

I have wandered about Qinghai's vast dominion

Only for the harvest season of the highland barleys.

It is for March's rain shed from the far-flung sky,

And May's flowers running rife on the parterre of the plateau,

That now the wind blows waves into the ripening crops.

The snow peaks are guardians of your untainted spirit,

And the mountain wind blows strength into your candid bosom.

Row after row of golden grains

Bow down their ears in tribute to the nurturing sun,

Their awns in tears of love for the tender, caring moon.

With ten thousand acres cavorting in the bliss of autumn,

And ten thousand wine cups clinking to their hearts' content,

Sleepless is the grassland tonight.

The bonfire lighting up half the sky

Will ignite songs of toast sweeping across the land like a wild storm.

雨中的查查香卡

陈劲松

路过这里的
除了我们的两辆汽车之外
还有几只蝴蝶和一群蜜蜂
以及，一场
七月末的大雨

小镇阒寂无声
静默生出了
幽暗而阔大的
倒影

我们在野外无边的油菜花海边停下
那些清澈的花香
掏出路过的人胸中
晦暗的部分

小驻之后，我们继续赶路
查查香卡，留在原地
一切静默依旧
它们都在等待着时间
把这场大雨
变换成一场严霜

TOWN OF CHACHA XIANGKA IN THE RAIN

Chen Jinsong

Whirling by this place
Were our two vehicles
Plus some butterflies and a swarm of bees,
In addition to
The midsummer shower.

The town was dead quiet,
Out of which was born
An looming shadow
Of dimness.

We stopped by the boundless sea of rapeseed flowers in the wild
Where the brisk scent of the flowers
Would purge any passersby
Of their hearts' heaviness.

After a brief sojourn, we went on our way, leaving
Chacha Xiangka where it was.
All was quiet, all was calm,
Awaiting the passage of time,
And summer's showers
To become thick winter frost.

车过贵德黄河大桥

东岳

我平生第一次看到
滚滚东去的黄河之水
竟是碧绿色的
（简直不对嘛）
她干净得
那么纯粹
仿佛少女
让我坚信

天下所有的
不论是已经逝去的
还是已经变得干枯的母亲
一定都曾经拥有过
一个如此华丽的清澈的
少女之身

CROSSING THE YELLOW RIVER BRIDGE AT GUIDE

Dong Yue

For the first time in life

Did I see the billowing Yellow River

In jade green

(How could that be ?)

Pure in her

Cleanliness,

Pristine like a maid,

Confirming to me

The once beautiful and

Clear virginity

All mothers under the sun

—Whether deceased

Or now still alive—

Had once had.

青海湖

海岸

QINGHAI LAKE

Hai An

悬于高原之巅，天色苍茫
湖水无边，爱无度
风声穿越于宁静之上

曾经哗啦啦的一棵棵大树
一根根脆脆响的芦苇
随远古漫漫的水路
在湖心沉落

四季变换的大湖，沉重
波纹隐藏的明镜
一圈又一圈
击碎地质的记忆

岁月的裂缝透不出回声
时光重重叠叠
生死一瞬间
一排排浪，绵绵不息

心不变，海的气息不曾改变
即便悬于海拔，悬于高原之巅
纵然远离大洋，远离光阴一万年
时光重重叠叠
生死一瞬间
一排排浪，绵绵不息

心不变，海的气息不曾改变
即便悬于海拔，悬于高原之巅
纵然远离大洋，远离光阴一万年

Overhung above the plateau.

Overcast, the boundless deep, like boundless love.

Whose quietude is transcended solely by the wind.

The trees erstwhile,

Reeds clacking one by one,

Without a trace, eons of evolution,

Ended up at the bottom of the lake.

A great lake, from out our Bourne of Time and Place, weighing heavily,

On the bright mirror with hidden ripples,

Ring after ring;

Geological memories fractured.

The crevices wrought by time, without echo,

Piled up relentlessly.

In an instant which means life and death,

Waves wash the cold shores as ever !

Certitude of sentiment, unaltered breath of the sea

Even as it rises yonder, climbing heavenward,

Exulting in a distance from the oceans, light years away in between.

茶卡·尼尔基

吴颖丽

茶卡，
你让我更加想念尼尔基。
你初秋八月的浩瀚，
让我格外想念尼尔基的烟波连天。
你积淀着青藏高原的深蓝，
恰似笼盖着尼尔基湖水的天空深情漫卷。

你那一池被赞颂经年的大青盐，
那人间烟火轻苦以及微甜之源，
让我想起故乡之湖尼尔基的水电，
点亮氤氲的街灯和窗棂以及尘世的顾盼，
却只是蕴含只是恩典，
只是默默无言。

而你身边的藏族蒙古族以及土族和撒拉族的笑脸，
让我更加想念自己的达斡尔亲眷，
想念他们拥我回乡时那亲切的语言，
就像人们把你唤作"茶卡"唤作"达布逊淖尔"，
我的亲眷们称我是"妞妞"——一个回来了的女孩，
在他们的心里，我从未走远。

茶卡，
你让我更加想念尼尔基。
你这深得有些神秘的夜空之镜，
让我格外想念尼尔基那星光拂面的夜晚。
你辉映着完颜通布和旺尕秀的雪峰之灵，
照见了我故乡的神山那莫力达瓦的伟岸。

CHAKA-NIRGI: A TALE OF TWO TOWNS

Wu Yingli

Chaka,

You really give me a pang of nostalgia for my home in Inner Mongolia.

Your early autumn's bounty

Makes me think of Nirgi's misty skyline.

Your turquoise blue of the highlands' essences

Resembles Lake Nirgi's canopy of the swirling skies.

Your reservoir of rock salt, worshipped over the years,

Enlightens the world's taste buds of life's ups and downs:

It reminds me of Nirgi's giant power dam

Fueling the misty street lamps, illuminating the window lattices and the

world's eager gazes

With multitudinous blessings

Of silence.

Surrounded by smiling faces—Tibetan, Mongol, Mongour, Salar—

You make me homesick for my Daur kinsmen,

For their endearing words of greeting on my homecomings.

Just as the people call you "Chaka" or "Dabusun Nor",

So too my kinsmen call me "Niu Niu" —a loving appellation for a home-coming girl

Who never has run away from their hearts.

Chaka, you really give me

A pang of nostalgia for my home in Nirgi.

Your mysterious mirror of the starry skies

Make me think of Nirgi's starlit nights.

Your mountain deities at the peaks of the Wanyan Tongbu and the Wanggaxiu

But echo the eloquence of the Morin Dawaa, a sacred mountain of my province.

湟水

周存云

HUANGSHUI RIVER

Zhou Cunyun

这是从高原走来的河流	A river ambles down the highlands
在青海之东	In the east of Qinghai,
她穿越了 370 多公里的生命历程	Traversing its 370−some−kilometre lifespan.
养育了众多的村庄之后	After nourishing sundry villages along its way,
汇入一条更大的河	It merges into a mightier flow.
她始终像母亲那样关注我	Though always tending to my needs as a mother does
陪伴我幼小的日子	Throughout my tenderest years,
直到把我推向成熟的生活	She nevertheless pushed me on to maturity
在河湟广阔的田野	Blooming in the Hehuang Valley's croplands.
我突然觉得	Then I suddenly found myself
自己就是一朵生长的葵花	A sprawling sunflower,
是众多种子中的一颗	One of the many burgeoning seeds in the wild.
淡黄的菊花　玫瑰色的大丽花	Pale yellow chrysanthemums and roseate dahlias
盛开宁静的秋天	Quietly bloom in the fall,
使我小小的庭院充满生命的光辉	Filling my patch of the land with a vibrant glow.
至今　我依然清楚地记得	To this day, I still remember
那个时代酸楚的农业	The struggles of the husbandry of yore
苦难就像一块块补丁	Conspicuously defacing my mother's dirty sleeves
醒目地布满母亲的衣袖	With patches of pain.
许多不知名的夜晚想起她	On many nameless nights she crossed my mind,
我就会有一种潮湿	Choking my heart with
一种潮湿中升起的疼痛	An agony arising out of the damp.
我的母亲般的河流啊	Oh, my mother—like consolation of a river,
有多少苦难	Where as much trouble lies
就有多少流淌的希望	As there does flowing hope!
当生命的车轮留下粗重的经络	And as the wheel of life inevitably leaves behind some heavy rut,
你家园般的恩情啊	So your homelike ways without fail
总让我产生莫名的感激	Leave me with a gratitude which I can never explain.

天鹅

郭建强

冬天，天鹅远来，栖居青海湖。她们在雪原冰湖的姿影和声息，像玉髓瑙石，不时入梦。

——题记

1

从夜半持久的梦的高度突然警醒
寒风泼洗车体，撩拨羊毛围巾，路灯通红
还没有到达你的领地
清亮的嗽鸣已经潜入昏沉的行旅

2

被度母护持的骨质宝瓶
盛载着古奥的密语驶向另一种古奥
天鹅叠压着白雪的翎羽梳理着空气
湖面收藏重新编织的美的变幻纹理

3

早就预感到天鹅的鸣唱会划出怎样的流线
丽达欢爱时的手指在唤起背脊留下的温柔和疼痛
等待了多长时间？如果不遇，我还会是我吗
顶着微燃的头颅、脖颈和身躯，沉思的香烛忘了自己

4

你们都将是天鹅眸中淡淡的流云
天鹅用无所在意又时时省察的灵息吐纳天地
你我将在天鹅的滑行中，交换彼此的内心地理学
错杂地交织另一只天鹅的幻影

SWANS

Guo Jianqiang

Swans alight by the Koko Nor in the winter, haunting my dreamland with graceful gait and soft sibilance, beautiful like chalcedony and agate.

—From the poet

1

Alerted by the midnight's dreamy altitude, I sensed

The cold wind abluting the vehicles and molesting my woolen scarf, and the traffic lights glowing like red lanterns.

I am not on your turf yet.

The wind's shrill cries have infiltrated the travelers' drooping hearts.

2

Bone−crafted treasure bottles blessed by Tārā

Convey the esoteric mantras towards another something esoteric.

The swans comb the air with snow−white plumes beneath their bodies;

The lake is in love with the kaleidoscopic patterns woven time after time.

3

Long have I anticipated the beautiful trajectories which the swans would draw with their singing;

Leda's fondling fingers evoked some residual softness and pain on their curvaceous contours.

How long have I been waiting？ Will I still be myself if we don't chance to meet？

With its scented head, neck and body aglimmer, the candle is lost in musing.

4

You will be like the wandering clouds to the swans,

Who breathe in and out the universe, knowingly or not.

Through their graceful glide, you and I will exchange our inner geographies,

Weaving out the apparition of another swan.

藏北帖

原上草

青藏呼哨季风，有深秋味道
植物嫩黄叶尖窥探
野碧桃难耐寂寞急于掏出深红
花蕾，被寒风擦燃

疾行。轰鸣抬高海拔，凛冽风声
穿过峡谷和村舍，残雪斑驳
荒野空旷，青玉河水，有冰块浮沉
若青稞琼浆，沉醉旷野
柳梢憋得通红，春讯沿河散布
牦牛不急不躁，眺望远处雪峰
然后低头，啃食冰碴草根

藏北，村落在积雪中静坐，牧羊人
斜戴皮帽裹紧头颅，坐在背风墙角
阳光踩踏万物走动
蓝空惊悸，有云丝轻拂
杨树仍旧抱紧枝条，版画样赤裸修行

皑皑山脉，如银蛇盘踞，如长云辉映
苍茫稀释烦闷，牧歌清脆
此刻，雪峰蜂拥而来，蓝空明净
我被凛冽搂抱，身躯燃烧

藏北，我久居的栖所
远处蓝湖里，有婴儿杂乱的呼叫
那是我散养的圣地精灵——
一群群白色的天鹅

A NOTE FROM THE CHANGTANG, OR NORTH TIBET

Yuan Shang Cao

O,The wind whistles across the Tibetan Highlands in the height of autumn;

The plants bud with yellow tentacles of tender leaves.

The wild peaches blossom, and, impatient of obscurity, put on a crimson color.

The flower buds are stricken afire in the cold wind.

A roar of the Earth has elevated the tableland. The cold wind's howl

Shoots through the valley with hamlets. The piebald snow thaws

In the barren. A jade—colored river, bobbing with ice,

Pours drunkenly on the plain like a highland barley nectar.

The willow twigs are swollen in red, harbingering the spring's arrival.

The yaks leisurely behold the distant snow peaks.

Lowering their heads, they gnaw at the ice—crisp roots of grass.

Snowy North Tibet finds its villages in meditative mood. A shepherd,

His leather hat aslant, sits snugly in the wall's lee.

The sun journeys through the day with all creation underfoot.

The blue sky throbs with gossamer wisps of clouds,

And the poplar trees shiver with stilted twigs, stiff as in a woodblock print.

The pristine ridges, capped with snow and serpentine, echo one another like the barring clouds,

Relieving my cares at once with their pastoral songs.

At this moment, I feel embraced by the mountains upon mountains

Ablaze in the burning chill beneath the clear blue sky.

North Tibet, my eternal abode!

Far out in the sapphire lake, I hear a cry of infants—

My bevy of swans,

Sundry sprites of the sacred land.

金子海

马丁

金子海不是金子的海
是比金子还要金贵的
水的湖泊，被湖泊滋养着的
八百里瀚海一方绿洲

风吹草低
远处是羊，更远是马
羊是云朵似的白羊
马是很多人梦中的白马
谁与媲配

不是风在吹。是绿衣红冠的
芦苇在潮涌。不是芦苇在荡
是过客一厢情愿的微醉
以致眩晕

是风在吹。蓝天白云下
这绿衣红冠的精灵
只接受水的滋润
风的日夜抚爱

是风在吹
水在暗流
金子海

JINZIHAI, A SEA OF GOLD

Ma Ding

Jinzihai Lake is no mere sea of gold;
It is a sea of something dearer:
Water. Plus a desert oasis
Fed by the lake.

The grass yields to the wind, unveiling
The distant sheep, and horses further out
—White sheep shaped like clouds,
And white horses that often haunt your dreams,
Unrivaled in handsomeness.

It is not the wind that is blowing, but the surging reeds
Crowned in red and clad in green; it is not the reeds that are
swaying,
But the hangover of a traveler that is causing
Such dizziness.

But it is the wind that is blowing. Under the blue sky smudged
with the white clouds,
These sprites of red and green
Can only be nurtured by the water
And fondled day and night by the wind.

The wind is blowing, and
The water is flowing silently in
The Sea of Gold.

放下了

伊沙

看见雪山我没有放下
那处女一样的雪山
也没能让我放下
看见黄河我没有放下
天下黄河青海清了
也没能让我放下
放不下
放不下
塔尔寺里有一千盏
酥油灯的神圣
一名紫红大袍的藏僧
抡动着肌肉饱满的大臂
鼓声滚滚而来
震破我缺氧的
心以及灵魂
我还是放不下
只是——
当我结束了此次远行
回到家中
手中的圆珠笔
在笔记本里追踪着
这首诗的时候
一切都放下了
该放下的
和不该放下的
统统被我放下了

GREAT RELIEF AT LAST

Yi Sha

Too much natural treats are served up during this tour

That I simply cannot ease into the pristine rhythms of wild Qinghai.

Its top sights range from the snow-capped mountains wreathed in mist.

Pure like a virgin.

To the landmark waterway— the Yellow River.

Both at their maximum crystal clear—I mean the river and the region.

Let alone the jaw-dropping landscapes in between.

Touched indeed that I don't want to miss out on any!

So many seductive, otherworldly panoramas.

So many views are stupefying.

Staring out through the silent five centuries of Tibetan Buddhism in

Ta'er Monastery.

Lit by sanctified butter lamps.

A Tibetan monk with a purple robe.

Swinging his muscular arms.

The sound of drums rumbling.

Overwhelming my heart and soul

Dazzled by lack of oxygen.

I still don't want to miss out on any thing, view, wonder on offer!

Finally I have eased into the leisurely rhythms of routine;

When back home,

In my cozy home.

A ball pen in hand.

Brainstorming starts from checking out my notebook.

In this poem being composed,

Everything falls into place.

Each excitement, placed into perspective.

Yes, I haven't missed out on nothing.

Great relief at last.

日记

海子

姐姐，今夜我在德令哈，
夜色笼罩
姐姐，我今夜只有戈壁
草原尽头我两手空空
悲痛时握不住一颗泪滴
姐姐，今夜我在德令哈
这是雨水中一座荒凉的城
除了那些路过的和居住的
德令哈……今夜
这是唯一的，最后的，抒情
这是唯一的，最后的，草原
我把石头还给石头
让胜利的胜利
今夜青稞只属于他自己
一切都在生长
今夜我只有美丽的戈壁空空
姐姐，今夜我不关心人类，
我只想你

DIARY

Hai Zi

O, my love, night falls on this desert town.

The train to Lassa pulls in to Delingha.

And I am as desolate as this Gobi Station.

The grasslands have ended but my grief holds

Like drought.

My hands an empty bowl.

My love, I am stranded here in Delingha—

Barren and wretched in the rain.

There's no one much about;

I watch others pass on trains.

O, Delingha, starkest grassland—world's last place, I am as

empty as you.

I give the stones back to the stones.

Let victory belong to those who win it.

Tonight each barley stalk belongs to itself entirely, and all

creation flourishes.

But I am alone with this merciless, beautiful desert town.

And I care for no one anywhere, but you.

河床
——《青藏高原的形体》之一
昌耀

我从白头的巴颜喀拉走下。

白头的雪豹默默卧在鹰的城堡，目送我走向远方。

但我更是值得骄傲的一个。

我老远就听到了唐古特人的那些马车。

我轻轻地笑着，并不出声。

我让那些早早上路的马车，沿着我的堤坡，鱼贯而行。

那些马车响着刮木、像奏着迎神的喇叭，登上了我的胸脯。轮子跳动在我鼓囊囊的肌块。

那些裹着冬装的唐古特车夫也伴着他们的辕马谨小慎微地举步，随时准备拽紧握在他们手心的刹绳。

他们说我是巨人般躺倒的河床。

他们说我是巨人般屹立的河床。

是的，我从白头的巴颜喀拉走下。我是滋润的河床。我是枯干的河床。我是浩荡的河床。

我的令名如雷贯耳。

我坚实宽厚、壮阔。我是发育完备的雄性美。

我创造。我须臾不停地

向东方大海排泻我那不竭的精力。

我刺肤文身，让精心显示的那些图形可被仰观而不可近狎。

我喜欢向霜风透露我体魄之多毛。

我让万山洞开，好叫钟情的众水投入我博爱的襟怀。

THE RIVERBED, THE FIRST OF THE POEM SERIES MANY FIGURES OF THE PLATEAU

Chang Yao

Walking down the white-headed Bayan Har Mountains,

I was sent off by a white-headed snow leopard crouching in an eagle's fortress.

I was the one to be proud.

For I had heard from afar the horse-drawn carriages of the Tangut people,

And I smiled in silence.

I acquiesced as those early bird coachmen retraced my footsteps uphill,

Their vehicles clinking up my bosom like clarions at a religious festival,

Their wheels bobbing up and down on my sinews and brawn.

These winter-clad Tangut drivers shuffled tentatively alongside their wheelhorses,

Ready to tighten up their grip over the bridles at any precarious moment.

They said I am a giant riverbed that is supine.

They said I am a giant riverbed that is erect.

Sure. Sauntering down the Bayan Har, I am a moist riverbed.

And I am a dry riverbed. I am a mighty one.

And my name is deafening to your ear.

Stout, strong and sturdy, symbolizing masculine beauty in its full bloom,

I am constantly creating—this I must. I must

Unleash my indefatigable strength into the eastern ocean nonstop.

My tattooed physique is to be admired from afar but not tampered with;

I love to unveil to the frosty wind my hairy, husky form.

I opened up my myriad mountain caves, to let my beloved waters into my bounteous bosom,

Just as a father does to his children.

我是父亲。

我爱听兀鹰长喉。他有少年的声带。他的目光有少女的媚眼。他的翼轮双展之舞可让血流沸腾。

我称誉在我隘口的深雪潜伏达旦的那个猎人。

也同等地欣赏那头三条腿的母狼。她在长夏的每一次黄昏都要从我的阴影跋向天边的彤云。

也永远怀念你们——消逝了的黄河象。

我在每一个瞬间都同时看到你们。

我在每一个瞬间都表现为大千众相。

我是屈曲的峰峦。是下陷的断层。是切开的地峡。

是眩晕的飓风。

是纵的河床。是横的河床。是总谱的主旋律。

我一身织锦，一身珠宝，一身黄金。

我张弛如弓。我拓荒千里。

我是时间，是古迹。是宇宙洪荒的一片腭骨化石。是始皇帝。

我是排列成阵的帆墙。是广场。是通都大邑，是展开的景观。是不可测度的深渊。

是结构力，是驰道。是不可克的球门。

我把龙的形象重新推上世界的前台。

而现在我仍转向你们白头的巴颜喀拉。

你们的马车已满载昆山之玉，走向归程。

你们的麦种在农妇的胝掌准时地亮了。

你们的团圞月正从我的脐蒂升起。

我答应过你们，我说潮汛即刻到来，

而潮汛已经到来……

I love to listen to the vulture's cries, whose youthful vocal cords and ogles of maiden coy move mountains,

Whose whirling dance of the wings stir up my bloodstreams.

I laud the huntsman awaiting his prey in my narrow mountain pass,

As well as the three-legged she-wolf limping in the snow,

Hobbling towards the twilight clouds at every dusk in the long summer.

So do I miss you—the Yellow River elephant now vanished from the planet's surface.

I see you all simultaneously, at every single moment.

I manifest as a myriad sentient beings at any given moment.

I am the mountains on mountains of crooked shapes, I am the submerged fault lines of the earth, I am the gaping isthmuses, and the giddy storms.

I am the Riverbeds, running straight and sideways, the theme melody of the symphony.

I—a body clad in embroidery, adorned with jewelry, aglitter with gold;

Versatile like a crossbow, bold like a thousand-mile horse.

I am time. I am the ancient relics. I am a piece of fossil bearing witness to the Creation. I am the First Emperor.

A wall of sails lined up in array. I am a city plaza; a giant metropolis; I am a panorama unrolled.

I am an unfathomable abyss. I am the power of physical structures. I am a highway, and an unconquerable goal.

I have reintroduced the dragon blazon to the world.

Yet now I still revert to your hoary-headed Bayan Har.

Your horse-drawn carriages, loaded with jades of the Kunlun Mountains, set out for home.

Your wheat fields are sprouting through the farm girl's calloused palms in good time.

Your rotund moon is being born from my navel cord.

I have promised you the coming of the spring tides—

And here they come.

在哈尔盖仰望星空

西川

有一种神秘你无法驾驭

你只能充当旁观者的角色

听凭那神秘的力量

从遥远的地方发出信号

射出光来，穿透你的心

像今夜，在哈尔盖

在这个远离城市的荒凉的

地方，在这青藏高原上的

一个蚕豆般大小的火车站旁

我抬起头来眺望星空

这时，河汉无声，鸟翼稀薄

青草向群星疯狂地生长

马群忘记了飞翔

风吹着空旷的夜也吹着我

风吹着未来也吹着过去

我成为某个人，某间

点着油灯的陋室

而这陋室冰凉的屋顶

被群星的亿万只脚踩成祭坛

我像一个领取圣餐的孩子

放大了胆子，但屏住呼吸

OUT INTO THE DISTANCE,
GAZING AT THE STARRY SKIES IN HAERGAI

Xi Chuan

Enveloping the world is a spirit beyond my ken.

I am left alone, gaping in bewilderment;

And succumbing to the mystery;

That blinks from somewhere as far as furthest can go;

Emitting signals from afar,

And radiating a light that pierces through my heart.

Tonight, in a desert called Haergai:

From the desolate, far−flung reaches of civilization;

In proximity to a namesake train station;

The size of a broad bean, on the Qinghai−Tibet Plateau;

That I look up into the starry skies.

The Milky Way's immensity remains mute as ever,

Under which birds are hardly seen in flight;

Grass grows rank up towards the stars,

While horses forget to take their wings.

The wind blows across the waste over the empty night,

Towards my future, and into my past.

Now I become someone, a shanty lit by an oil lamp,

Whose freezing roof is trampled under the myriad stars;

Into a sacrificial altar.

I become a child partaking of the Lord's Supper:

While holding my breath, mindful of my trembling.

嘉那嘛呢石的星空

吉狄马加

　　"嘛呢"来自梵文佛经《六字真言经》"唵嘛呢叭咪哞"的简称,因在石头上刻有"嘛呢"而称"嘛呢石";"嘛呢堆"是指在石板或经加工而成的石头上刻有藏文经文、"六字真言"或刻有动物图纹、神灵图像、朗久旺丹图纹等的石板或石头垒起来的石堆。青海省玉树地区结古镇新寨村,有一座石头堆成的锥形小山,名叫"嘉那嘛呢石"。青海的许多村镇都有这样的石堆,而结古镇新寨村的这座石堆最大最高,它占地2.4万平方米,高3米,25—26亿块石头,成为众石堆中的"翘楚"。300多年前,藏传佛教的嘉那活佛在这里放下了第一块刻有藏文经文的石头。之后,信佛教的老百姓追随嘉那活佛,都在这里放下了刻有经文的石头,这个石堆也即以"嘉那"命名。信众们相信嘛呢石都具有神圣的意义和神秘的力量。因之成了青南地区(康巴,安多)广大信徒朝拜的一方圣地。

THE STARRY SKIES OVER THE JIANA MANI STONES MOUND

Jidi Majia

　　Mani stones are stone plates, rocks and/or pebbles, carved or inscribed with the six syllabled mantra of Avalokiteshvara (Om mani padme hum, hence the name "Mani stone"), as a form of prayer.In Xinzhai Village, Jiegudo Town, 800 km south of Xining,capital of Qinghai Province, there is a cairn (conical hill of stones) called "Jiana Mani Stones". Such stony pilings either in form of pile or wall,under the influence of Tibetan Buddhism, are widely found in Qinghai and the one in Xinzhai Village,named after a certain Kham guru Jiana, counts the largest and tallest, covering an area of 24,000 square meters and is 3 meters in height, consisting of 2.5−2.6 billion stones. Legend has it that, 300 years ago, the Reverend placed the first tablet engraved with sutra and ever since then, generations upon generations of believers' relaying effort has formed the largest secret site that it is to the extent this compelling cairn has been attracting droves of pilgrims and tourists for the last 300 years. Standing in the shadow of mani stones, feeling their power and presence, it's impossible not to let your imagination run wild.

是谁在召唤着我们？

石头，石头，石头

那神秘的气息都来自于石头

它的光亮在黑暗的心房

它是六字真言的羽衣

它用石头的形式

承载着另一种形式

每一块石头都在沉落

仿佛置身于时间的海洋

它的回忆如同智者的归宿

始终在生与死的边缘上滑行

它的倾诉在坚硬的根部

像无色的花朵

悄然盛开在不朽的殿堂

它是恒久的纪念之碑

它用无言告诉无言

它让所有的生命相信生命

石头在这里

就是一本奥秘的书

无论是谁打开了首页

都会目睹过去和未来的真相

这书中的每一个词语都闪着光

雪山在其中显现

Who is it out there, beckoning us in the landscape of Southern Qinghai ?

It is the Jiana Mani Mound, erected in Jiegudo's countryside,

Grown over decades into a most iconic monument.

Permeated by a mystical breath.

A swirl of Tibetan Buddhist myths,

All in testament to Kham's modern-day piety,

Like a beam piercing through a Samsaric heart,

The flowery plumage of six-syllabled mantra,

Sacred, numinous utterances of wish fulfillment,

These stones make an offering to spirits of place;

Each stone weighs heavily,

As if it has tapped into the ocean of time,

Its memories, like the final moments before a Brahmin's death,

Teeter between life and death, beginning and end.

Each confesses a truth from its unfathomable depth.

Colorless flowers, bursting forth from the Chorten of Nirvana,

A case of an intentional process art.

This mind-boggling Oriental Stonehenge dominates wordlessly.

Proselytizing without sermon or text,

Attracting steady flows of pilgrims and tourists,

Who walk this holy corner across the vast territory of Qinghai.

It pays dividends to peruse this colossal parchment, another Dead Sea Scroll!

Whoever thumbs through its first page,

Before he blows out his desires and gains Moksha, deliverance from Samsara.

Look, how every rock sparkles, talismanically,

Mirroring the snowy mountains in the distance.

光明穿越引力，蓝色的雾霭

犹如一个飘渺的音阶

每一块石头都是一滴泪

在它晶莹的幻影里

苦难变得轻灵，悲伤没有回声

它是唯一的通道

它让死去的亲人，从容地踏上

一条伟大的旅程

它是英雄葬礼的真正序曲

在那神圣的超度之后

山峦清晰无比，牛羊犹如光明的使者

太阳的赞辞凌驾于万物

树木已经透明，意识将被遗忘

此刻，只有那一缕缕白色的炊烟

为我们证实

这绝不是虚幻的家园

因为我们看见

大地没有死去，生命依然活着

黎明时初生婴儿的啼哭

是这片复活了的土地

献给万物最动人的诗篇

嘉那嘛呢石，我不了解

这个世界上还有没有比你更多的石头

因为我知道

你这里的每一块石头

都是一个不容置疑的个体生命

Light defies gravity, and a blue mist,

Plays like an ethereal musical scale.

The presence of this Tennessee jar-like pile inspires awe;

Each stone represents a teardrop, in its crystalline shape,

Having afflictions alleviated, misdeeds exonerated.

This is the sole path to Buddhahood,

An easy passage to Heaven for the departed.

In a real overture to a hero's funeral,

When no more hindered by desires, fettered by ignorance,

The summits become exceedingly clear.

The sheep and cattle flock as bearers of light,

While odes of the sun soar above all creation.

The trees turn transparent; consciousness fades into oblivion.

At this moment of truth, only the endless wisps of white smoke,

Testify to the vibrancy of this imposing structure.

Look, how life goes on as the Earth exists.

The early-morning cries of the newborn,

Dedicate a most moving poem to all the sentient beings.

O Jiana Mani stones, I have the foggiest idea

Whether one will ever find a more impressive mound in this world.

One thing is for sure—

Each stone is a searching soul wandering at the threshold of Nirvana.

它们从诞生之日起

就已经镌刻着祈愿的密码

我真的不敢去想象

二十五亿块用生命创造的石头

在获得另一种生命形式的时候

这其中到底还隐含着什么?

嘉那嘛呢石,你既是真实的存在

又是虚幻的象征

我敢肯定,你并不是为了创造奇迹

才来到这个世界

因为只有对每一个个体生命的热爱

石头才会像泪水一样柔软

词语才能被微风千百次的吟诵

或许,从这个意义上而言

嘉那嘛呢石,你就是真正的奇迹

因为是那信仰的力量

才创造了这超越时间和空间的永恒

Ever since you rose from your obscure origin,

When your first rock was inscribed with the famed Avalokitesvara mantra,

Each syllable painted in a symbolic color,

You have begun to grow exponentially,

Until my wildest guess fails to take stock of your size,

A most wonderous marvel in an era of unfaith.

What a massive stone sprawl!

Symbol of insight into impermanence and anatta, or non-self!

And embodiment of all the faithfuls,

Impatient of the joys and frustrations of six realms of cyclic rebirths—

I dare say to you:

You were not painstakingly born the land's most enduring puzzle piece.

Without the Bodhisattvas' compassion for all,

Your stones would not have become so velvety, like,

Tears blowing out desires and gaining the truth about Dharma,

Letting the breeze chant those six sweet sounds over and over.

It is perhaps in this sense, that ;

You are nothing short of a miracle, a modern healing ground.

It is the sheer spiritual power in you,

The unswerving faith in your inherent wish fulfilment;

That has wrought such a cumulative achievement, sitting no more in splendid isolation.

沿着一个方向，嘉那嘛呢石
这个方向从未改变，就像刚刚开始
这是时间的方向，这是轮回的方向
这是白色的方向，这是慈航的方向
这是原野的方向，这是天空的方向
因为我已经知道
只有从这里才能打开时间的入口
嘉那嘛呢石，在子夜时分
我看见天空降下的甘露
落在了那些新摆放的嘛呢石上
我知道，这几千块石头
代表着几千个刚刚离去的生命
嘉那嘛呢石，当我瞩望你的瞬间
你的夜空星群灿烂
庄严而神圣的寂静依偎着群山

As custom of solstice and ritual dictates;

You should be circumvented from the left side,

The clockwise direction in which the earth and the universe revolve,

And so be it—the direction of reincarnation likewise;

The color of white, the port where Compassion and Mercy set sails.

Where we come to unravel the essence of Being and ponder the nature of Void,

Take in the unforgettable atmosphere of a replica of Jerusalem Syndrome—

The feeling of intense emotion experienced by pilgrims,

On their first sighting of the Holy Site.

I surmise you might serve as a possible entrance into time.

In the midnight, I see sweet dewdrops fall from the sky,

On those new arrivals,

These additions, some argue:

Auguring the newly departed return to their spirit home.

As you operate diachronically from light to darkness, from day to night.

I behold your constellations glitter in the firmament,

While an august stillness reigns supreme far and wide.

远处的白塔正在升高

无声的河流闪动着白银的光辉

无限的空旷如同燃烧的凯旋

这时我发现我的双唇正离开我的身躯

那些神授的语言

已经破碎成无法描述的记忆

于是，我仿佛成为了一个格萨尔传人

我的灵魂接纳了神秘的暗示

嘉那嘛呢石，请你塑造我

是你把全部的大海注入了我的心灵

在这样一个蓝色的夜晚

我就是一只遗忘了思想和自我的海螺

此时，我不是为吹奏而存在

我已是另一个我，我的灵魂和思想

已经成为了这片高原的主人

嘉那嘛呢石，请倾听我对你的吟唱

虽然我不是一个合格的歌者

但我的双眼已经泪水盈眶！

The distant white pagoda ascends,

The river meanders and ripples silver,

The boundless Void triumphs like a flaming torch.

In this moment, I feel like my lips are parting from my body,

All the divine verbal resources, by and for humans,

Have evaporated without a trace.

Therefore, I seem to have become an inspired Gesar oral bard.

My soul, in a trance, my tongue, improvising on end.

Jiana Mani Stones, I pray;

To carve me, inscribe any devotional designs on me;

Pour the whole ocean into my spirit,

On a blue night like tonight,

It is the vast and the boundless in you,

The ultimate Compassion and Mercy of Bodhisattva;

That makes me shrink by fractions, a mere senseless conch.

In this moment, I deem myself no more a worthy singer,

As I'm a different self; my soul and thoughts;

Have at last merged into this plateau.

In my chanting of Om mani padme hum,hymn to Higher Beings,

I prostrate, humbled into an awareness;

All my vocal effort is but soundless throbbing,

While my eyes brim over with tears.